# NADA

a novel by TONKO

McBussy Publishing

All rights reserved.

Copyright © Tonko, 2026

No portion of this book may be reproduced in any form without written permission from the publisher or author, except as permitted by U.S. copyright law.

The author may be reached at tonko.nada@gmail.com; the publisher may be reached at mcbussypublishing@gmail.com, or find them in the Mommy Dom VRChat Roleplay server (which they moderate).

Cover design by Matt Margolis: @exittstarr, mattmmargolis@gmail.com

For a dream woman.

"It is the universal testimony that there is nothing in the character of the nadanian which is opposed to the humanian. They possess all the higher attributes of the mind; their perceptions of religion and their sense of moral obligations are just; their imagination is fertile; their aptitude for instruction, and their powers for imitation are great; neither are they wanting in a desire to improve their condition; they are sensible of the superiority of the humanians, and of the disadvantages under which they themselves labour, from their want of knowledge, and the converted nadanians are generally very anxious for the education of their children. The chief obstacles to the advancement of nadanians are their want of self-dependence, and their habits of indolence, which have been fostered, if not created, by the policy of the Universal Government..."

- **The Gomez Report, 174 PC**

"Every square inch of every piece of land in this asteroid belt and across the great sapper is nadanian land."

- **Franette Longdoor, Universal Government First Ahket, Assembly of Nadanian Ahkets, 353PC**

# Prologue

I have a question for you, and so this is my question, and it's something I'm pretty upset about, you're going to get some pretty hard questions and discussions, but you have to remember: this is our land.

I can't find medicines anymore. You have to understand this because these things you're telling me, quill harvesting, for all I'm concerned you're cutting out the heart of the asteroid, you're cutting out the heart of Nada. Tell me this: can you survive without a heart? You're destroying the spirit of Nada, the great sapper. You're destroying the soul of the asteroid. I know you may not want to hear this but I'm telling you.

Our harvesting of molerin has gone down drastically. You're lucky if you can even find them there anymore. You opened a killing zone for molerin. Now we lost our molerin. That was their vegetation, you know? We keep telling you. We have to live here. What's left for molerin? We have to live here. You're impacting the life of the asteroid. They all work together, that one and that one and that one, and if you impact one you impact them all. Air is life. You like air? Fresh air?

I have little ones coming. All of you up there have to understand this. You got little ones coming. Air is life, all you ought to realize this. They're the lungs of the great sapper. You have to realize that this is our lives. You're strangling the great sapper. Some will get rich but you're killing the rest of us.

As far as our ahkek goes, and he's close with your Government, and so am I – I run six programs so I know what I'm talking about – and he's a very spiritual and guided individual. So when I say these things, know that they aren't just words. These things are real. Everything has spirit. And the minister, he knows this; he'll tell you the same things.

Look at the benefits – what do we get out of this? We live here, and you guys get rich taking all the quills. What will happen to our asteroid now? We got nothing. Maybe two or three guys working. That's nothing. You're just going to let us die. All you care about is killing.

I don't care whether you like it or not, but this is the bottom line. This is what we have to put up with as nadanians. You guys come here and you cut up all the quills and then you leave. But we're stuck here. You got to understand this. Where can we go? What do we get? Nothing. Maybe three or four guys working.

And then there's the sacred items that have gone missing from over there, and you guys know what I'm talking about. And you guys start messing with our stuff – that's total disrespect. And you guys want to talk about respect? That's where I'm coming from. You have to show us respect.

I sat here and listened to you all morning. And it may seem like I'm angry, but it's out of respect because you guys should have respect for us as nadanians. You guys are out in treaty area. Remember that while you're standing there.

I'm also known as a very respected ahkek, so I know what I'm talking about, and I sit on the nadanian asteroidal ahkek committee with others across Nada. That's why it's important to be here. That's why I'm telling you the things I'm telling you. There's ahkek across Nada, in Gar-Nada, right across Nada, and I said to them, like, what do you guys have to offer? To give us back? You're taking millions – billions – and then you leave us in the dark. With no air. With no molerin. We're sick of that. We get nothing. Maybe four or five guys quilling. How many billions of dollars do you get from quills? That's what I'm talking about. And are you even listening? I'm an ahkek, and nadans listen to me. The minister in your government listens to me.

Our crabbing is gone. Our asteroidal... Medicinal medicines, because I work with medicines, and so put that in your statement that I talked with your biologist. Because I'm a sapipe carrier, and that means I look into the other world, and so I know things that your biologist doesn't know. When are you going to show that respect because I think it's time. You guys got to show us respect. We give and give and give, but what do we get in return? Nothing.

So you have to look at all of that... Going back to quills... I was just in Rock Nippan and I said to them you made a killing zone for all the molerin. And you're still in Nada treaty land up here.

I live in Rock Nippan, in our natural home, because that's where our ahket originally was. That's all of our area. Don't underestimate me or disrespect me because I know a lot of our ahkeks that still live up here. And I keep telling you.

You know, green is one thing. And us as ahkek nadanians, we look out at everything growing around us, right? Where was that equal revenue sharing that was signed with the Universal Government?

You know, we talk about our nadanian rights, and we never signed with Gar-Nada. We signed with the Universal Government. You guys got to understand the declaration on the rights of nadanians. We can tell you guys no-go Because Gar-Nada has no say over us. We didn't sign with Gar-Nada, we signed with the Universal Government.

I say this, and it's the truth.

I know a lot of nadanians that live in this whole area. That asteroid and that asteroid. And you're going to impact them. They're crabbing, and I'm damn sure they're not going to be happy. Because I know them. Because I talk to them.

And all of this quilling… I have a question to ask of you. Why don't you put it all on the table and show where you already have places you want to quill. I know you have other places. And that's respect, putting it all out there. Because I don't see it, and you're taking everything and you're hiding it from everyone. And I know this because I talk to nadanians, and nadanians talk to me because I'm ahkek.

You guys – we have an inheritance on our rights, on our asteroidal lands. And me, as a traditional ahkek, I sit on committees across Nada. I sat on a court. And we make a major impact on our country, on Nada.

The reason why I'm all upset is because you guys took everything and left us here with nothing. We didn't even get any kind of support or funding to help support our ahket. We get nothing from the government. And that ain't going to happen anymore. Enough is enough. We have to get something.

So, I'm asking you what you guys have to offer nadanians. You harvest quills and you're taking billions of dollars from us, and we end up with nothing. You come onto our asteroids that we use for crabbing and molerins and medicines. That's my gift, I'm able to tell you these things, and it's out of respect. That's what's happening here. That's why I'm putting all of this on the table. What do you guys have to offer us? What benefits do we get when you take all our money?

Is your CEO here? Your head guy? I'm going to press for an answer to that, because we are suffering. Why don't you guys give back some support to our ahket, you know, help our ahket in different areas. Because we get nothing, and we're suffering. I've never seen anyone bring that to us, to certain areas. Like housing. All of these things, but no, you guys just take a lot.

So that's the biggest question I'm asking you. And you can take that back to your CEO or whatever, but we want our funding and supports or something. That's what we're asking. We're not asking for your company. We're asking for supports. Financial supports, because you guys have tooken all that away from us. And you've given us back nothing, financial or otherwise.

I don't mean to be rude, but the truth is the truth, and you have to understand this. Because when you come in here I want you to understand that. As a nadanian, we're sick of being stepped on, and you're stepping on us. We're sick of you taking everything for granted from us, and it's time you guys start giving back. Because we get nothing.

I hope for damn sure that the minister does that, because he's a good friend of mine. And believe me, he'll hear about this.

You have to understand that we have health issues. There are many different organizations and we were never even offered any kind of support.

So there's that – like, how would you guys feel? Like, be honest, how would you feel? You sure as hell won't be doing any of this stuff, right? You have common sense, so use it.

We're getting caught up in the technology, and we're forgetting about life. Nadanian life. And as nadanians, we think about life. We think about it because we have to. You showed us a thing up there, a map or whatever of all of those quills. Every one of those quills, my friend, has a spirit. And these aren't just words, it's the truth. Each time you cut down a quill you're killing a spirit. Every quill gives us air. We're killing ourselves. I say this not as a nadanian, but everyone else is killing us. We are the land. We are the asteroid. And that's how we see it. Everything has a spirit and intent. And that's how us, as nadanians, accept it. We don't wipe it all out. We don't kill all the quills. We're killing ourselves.

And the reason why I'm upset about this, the reason why I seem like this, my friends, is I've got little ones, little nadanians; you've got little ones. And you have to think about those ones. Think about your descendants. Like, what kind of legacy are you leaving for them?

I know I might be upsetting you, but what I think about I talk about, and I talk about the issues that matter. And we know for a lot of people it stings and hurts like hell. But as a spiritualist and ahkek throughout Nada, I speak on behalf of the great sapper because it involves all of us. We're all part of the great sapper and we live on the great sapper, and without the great sapper none of us would be here, and so that's important. We start killing her, and we're killing ourselves. We're killing our little ones. There's no future.

I sat here listening to all of your presentation, and, to me, technology is killing us.

I'll share one thing I shared with this young lady, this humanian. How are medicines ever taken out of here? They're natural, you know, on the asteroids. They're not chemicals. And look at all the chemicals that are killing nadanians. Everything in Rock Nippan. Chemicals, alcohol and drugs – they're all killing nadanians. It's affecting every family, every ahket, in Nada. Not just in Rock Nippan or Gar-Nada – all of Nada. Chemicals. It's killing nadanians. It's killing our species. It's impacting on every ahket. And yet we have these natural medicines, we have all these spirits, in the quills, in the crabs, on splatfern, and these spirits are medicines. And they're natural medicines – you don't get hooked on it. It heals the body. It helps the body and spirit and mind, and you need all of that to be healthy. And nadanians aren't healthy. Look around you. Whereas technology kills the body and mind and spirit. These are two different things.

And so it's the same thing happening: you take, take, take. Killing everything. You're killing us with your technology. You're killing us with your chemicals.

I don't know how to explain it any better, but I'm going to tell you because you got to understand.

Another point I have for you, and maybe you should write this down, is there should be policies in place where only every so often – six years, I'll say, because six is important, because of the six ways – you should be quilling, not every year, not all the time. There should be a policy, and it should be mandatory, that you can only do it every so many years. So write that down in your books.

I know you have a lot of asteroids where you want to quill, not just here, but all over, and you should put that on the table, like I said. Because we need a little support financially. Why don't you guys give anything back? Because you took our crabbing, and you left us with nothing.

And that policy is a must, as far as I'm concerned. It's got to happen, buddy. Because this isn't going anywhere if it isn't.

And one other thing. In our organization, in our ahket, you're in treaty area. I'm a nadanian environmentalist, and so who is your environmentalist? That's what I'd like to know.

Why weren't we allowed to go out and do an environmental assessment of the asteroid? Because we know the plants – what you would call plants, but we know as spirits, and there's some that you don't even know about. But we know them. As nadanians, we know them. We know the medicines there. You don't know that. You're worried about things other than that. And that's what we've been dealing with: universities and everything, government.

When are you going to start respecting us as nadanians and start looking at us as environmentalists? Because we see things differently from you. Our ways of knowing are different. Because we live on the land, and, no disrespect, but I know you don't. You go to the store. Well, our store is the land, is the asteroid. We crab. We pick medicines. So, when are you going to put that perspective in your assessments? Because it's very different. For nadanians, for the ahket, for us that know the asteroids – for us to go out with you on the asteroid. Then maybe we'd get respect, but who knows.

And that's the thing: when are you going to start respecting the ahket as nadanians. We know where the medicines come from. You have no clue what we understand. Your science is not our science. We come at it from a different perspective.

I'm talking about – we're talking about – all this university stuff. But us as nadanians we have more meaning and understanding in the land, in the asteroid, than technology. Technology is worried about certain things, but it's not worried about us. You might see two or three things, but nadanians would see hundreds, thousands. For every plant or animal that's out there, my friend, it carries a spirit just like you and I. And we're spiritual people. That's something to respect. And we need that.

One more thing. Some of the medicines, they just aren't there anymore. Where you quill, there's nothing. I don't find anything, only bits and pieces of medicine. And that's what I mean, you have to go from here to up there. Where it was once right in our backyards now we have to go to other asteroids.

I went there with a biologist, and I actually live down there, in Rock Nippan, and I did an environmental inspection, and that's way over on another asteroid. And there's nothing there.

You have to understand about nadanian treaty and the asteroidal resources act. We signed with the Universal Government, we didn't sign with Gar-Nada. We'll fight you in court about that, you better believe that. The government of Gar-Nada was never supposed to be above us, because we signed treaty with the Universal Government. Government was supposed to be here, below us.

And I'll tell you, lady, that all that is bullshit. Look, the minister, I hope he kicks the shit out of all this bullshit that's been putting us down. And when that happens you'll know how it feels, and it ain't a damn good thing, lady. We've been going through this for hundreds of years, and it's bullshit.

Because you better look things up, lady. Nadanians, our ahket, we're starting to tear all of those walls down. Big time. And you damn well know that.

We're going to get rid of all that crap.

Because there's no asteroids that are supposed to be done in like you're saying it will be done in, there's no land available because under our asteroidal land entitlement there's no deals supposed to be done while we have that in place, and the Gar-Nada government should know that. Right? We can take anywhere we want. You guys can't give our asteroids away, not without coming to us.

You're infringing on our rights, on our entitlement. You're not supposed to be issuing anything unless it's brought forward and we're informed. Gar-Nada knows that. That's why we have the entitlement in place.

But we're kicking down the doors, lady. And it ain't gonna be good. And you know that.

*Pearson Decision, 320PC.* Ulah Pearson was convicted of illegal cloud crabbing because the nets he used were larger than his permit allowed. He argued that crabbing was a nadanian right, protected by the Universal Government's constitution. Courts sought to determine whether or not a nadanian right had been infringed upon, and, if so, whether or not the infringement was justified.

# 1

Liam Melnykczuk turned off his phone. He had been fired. Well, not quite fired, but it was a Saturday, and no one, especially someone who worked in a government office, called on a Saturday, not if it wasn't serious, which it almost certainly never was. Even if it approached the often-indeterminate definition of serious, in all likelihood, it could wait until, at least, 8:00AM on Monday morning. Really, no one has ever been fired from a government, union-protected position; no, they were admonished, they were disciplined, their roles, their duties-as-assigned, would be changed, their leash would be tightened, their collar choked, they'd be walked around the office, followed, led to and from the washroom. One could, Liam thought, climb up onto the photocopier, defecate into the loading tray, shoot out hundreds of copies of black-and-white-and-brown papers, which, if the papers were flipped through quickly enough, would animate the sludge as it worked its way into the machine's gears and crevices, never to be fully cleaned again. At most an out-of-order sign would appear, but one would certainly never be fired. As a public servant, to be fired required drinking and driving, multiple hit-and-runs, murder, or worse, sexualized cannibalism of entire dementia and/or young mothers' wards, during work hours.

Instead, he had been put on leave. No, that's not exactly right either – it had been suggested to him by his director that he take some time for himself, his director who, without a doubt, had been instructed to do so by the assistant deputy minister, who, equally so, had been instructed by the deputy minister, and so on and so forth. Where that instruction had begun, the seed of Liam's firing, its germination, could well have been with the minister of asteroidal resources.

Further, *taking time for himself* was a not-too-subtle euphemism for using up the rest of his vacation hours just as the fiscal year had begun, and, if need be (although this wasn't confided to him by his director, the director of quill harvesting, because Liam's transgressions were so egregious that they did not warrant confidence, not any longer) the director had hinted that he should use up the remainder of his accumulated sick time, too, and, if even that wasn't enough time for himself, leave without pay.

But for all intents and purposes, it was the same: Liam was, or would soon be, fired.

He sat back in his chair and looked down at the report he'd been reading on the desk in front of him when the director called, and it briefly occurred to him that he should finish writing it, but that feeling swiftly evaporated. He was, technically, it seemed, now on vacation, and, given that, and despite it being 9:30AM, he thought he should celebrate that fact, and so he poured himself a glass of nadanian red wine. It wasn't the best wine he'd ever had, he preferred the humanian varieties, vineyards from warmer worlds, but it did have a quality that Liam greatly appreciated: it was cheap, and, as such, he could buy it and drink it in large volumes.

He had never before been fired. Nothing so much as approached it. When he was younger, when he first started to work for the department of asteroidal resources, he was chastised, primarily for idleness, but, as Liam saw it, it was more that he had completed everything that was tasked of him and had vocalized his idleness, in the form of a query regarding the protracted approval of one of the quill harvesting management plans, which, or so Liam thought, showed both his interest and initiative in more complicated undertakings that the department oversaw, but that was not how it was received. Managers, especially managers whose job it is to ensure that their subordinates have an appropriate amount of work – work that consumes the majority of their 7.25 paid hourly day – are somewhat loath to be told that they aren't doing their job, which *was* how it was received. But aside from that, looking back, it was hardly anything at all.

Liam's performance, on the contrary, was one without flaw. He had, or so he thought, become an indispensable component for the proper and responsible management of Nada's voluminous quill resources. In fact, without him, without the introduction of improved approaches to resource management – approaches, fashionably called *sustainable quill harvesting*, that he developed and implemented across Nada – without which the protracted approval of a quill harvest licence, the licence for which he was chastised over, would, Liam was positively sure, still be under consideration, all these years later. It was just such ingenuity that allowed him to rise rank in the department, first as part of the field crew tasked with ensuring that harvested quills were returning, then as a lice management specialist, then as a remote asteroidal photoanalyst, then as acting-quill harvest planner, then as a full-time quill harvest planner, and then, finally, in the position to which, up until the phone call with his director, he held for many years, chief quill harvester. He developed policy and program directions, advised and briefed ministers and deputy ministers (many of whom have come and gone, under several governments, which, too, had come and gone), attended and presented at scientific conferences, sat as the government's representative on several boards, and, generally, had his fingers in as many pots as he had fingers, which included nadanian consultation.

And it was this last item, nadanian consultation, that Liam knew was the reason for his firing.

He opened the Quill-NADA report about his recent trip to Rock Sandbar and flipped to what he thought may be, if not the offending page, the offending sentiment. He read:

"Which brings me to nadanian data sovereignty. Quill-NADA has spent a lot of time focusing on this component, and they've brought in a company called Asteroidal Relations to produce a guide on how to acknowledge that the data collected by research scientists, like those very scientists in Quill-NADA, is nadanian data, and that that data is owned by the nadanians on whose asteroids – their 'ancestral' asteroids – it was collected. To Asteroidal Relations, and to many at Quill-NADA, nothing is not nadanian-owned data; that is to say: everything is nadanian data. Quill abundance data, species data, lice data, data on water and soil and air and fungal-plants and animals – everything is nadanian data. I'll even quote one of the speakers: 'Even remotely-sensed data is nadanian data.'

"Because this is nadanian data, and such nadanian data is sovereign, it is also the nadanians that control how that data can be used. And, given that this data is 'sovereign', given that it is 'nadanian-owned', I don't think it's a large leap that they would want to be compensated, monetarily, for using their data – for they own it, don't they? For they are sovereign, aren't they?

"Here's the definition: Sovereign (adjective): *possessing supreme or ultimate power.*

"Under Quill-NADA's nadanian data sovereignty framework, any data collected in Nada, on anything, is nadanian data. I think we should be cognizant that the nadanian data sovereignty movement is linked to the asteroidal reclamation movement, which is one of relinquishing the Universal Government's sovereignty and authority.

"If all data – on quills or otherwise, remotely sensed or otherwise – is sovereign nadanian data, then that has many larger implications. But, of course, no researcher is going to give up the data they themselves collected, and say 'I have no right to use this data that I collected in my research,' and they will certainly not pay someone else to use the data that they themselves collected and compiled and analyzed and are attempting to publish, and they will not be constrained in how they think that data can be used. And so, in practice, it is demonstrably *not* sovereign nadanian data, and we should not pretend, in some kind of obsequious fashion like this, that it is otherwise. It is, frankly, insulting."

He continued to read:

"The presiding speaker began to focus on one of the principal goals of Quill-NADA, which was to 'thread nadanian knowledge (or nadanian science, or nadanian ways of knowing, whatever one might call it) into their own quill-based, scientific research.'

"This was discussed as if it were one of the easiest things to accomplish, but I remain unconvinced. Quill-NADA is entering its third year of its Universally-funded five-year research program, and so if they intend to 'thread nadanian knowledge' into it, they better start threading. Because doing that is not easy. No one has a good definition of what nadanian knowledge is, let alone how to thread it into the framework of evidence-based science, with its hypothesis forming and testing, data gathering and compiling, analyzing and critiquing, and, if the results come up wanting, hypothesis dismissal. Nadanian knowledge, by contrast, contains elements of myth, religion, just-so stories. For instance, according to nadanian knowledge, the ratfruit is medicine for the heart. Why? Because the shape and colour of a ratfruit is similar to the shape and colour of a nadanian heart – and that is why nadanians call the ratfruit, the heart-fruit. No doubt nadanian knowledge does contain something valuable, but it, too, would need to be thrown into the serrating blades of the scientific process. And not everything survives.

"There is also an underlying, unsaid, borderline specist element to this: that nadanians can't do actual science, that they can only ever do 'science lite', that they are treated like children and can't follow the objectiveness, the rigidness of the scientific process – and instead, we are to be like proud parents, and put their crayon drawings on the fridge, happy with the knowledge that they're trying their best. This, pardon my humanian French, is bullshit. Nadanians, just like humanians, can do and contribute to the advancement of scientific knowledge.

"Perhaps my pessimism will be proved wrong – but I doubt that any nadanian knowledge will be threaded by the end of 360PC."

It was this kind of sentiment, a skeptical, some would call critical, others would call specist (although he would disagree with the latter) sensibility of nadanian ways of knowing, that had caused him to have this newfound abundance of 'time for himself'. It was not the first time he had voiced such criticism.

Liam threw the report in the garbage and poured himself another glass of wine.

There was, he must not forget, the episode that occurred during the completely voluntary inter-departmental office book club that Liam had joined. He was content to keep his computer's camera and audio off, eat his lunch, and stay silent, letting the others (from the department of transportation or justice or asteroid environmental safety or nadanian and humanian resources) do the talking. At least, that was what he intended to do, and intentions are only that: intentions.

The conversation was supposed to be about the history of nadanian colonization, the creation of the nadanian exploration company, the model declaration, the rock nippan treaty, the nadanian treaty, the gar-nada act, the alien act, the asteroidal resources act, the statement of the Universal Government on nadanian policy, the declaration on the universal rights of nadanians, and, if time permitted, the naman treaty. Instead, it turned into a collective guilt trip on all of the hurtful and trauma-inducing ways that humanians had inflicted misery upon the forever-suffering nadanians, who were, as they always were, victims of interstellar colonization with no sense of autonomy, incapable of making decisions for themselves, not to say that humanian decisions have always been for the better. Nadanians, just as everyone everywhere, have a history, and that history includes the simplex virus, which devastated nadanian communities, and to which the Universal Government was by no means unsympathetic.

True, the introduction of alcohol was of equal devastation, as more and more nadanians abandoned their traditional familial organization, which was, we must not forget, a single nadanian male with up to several dozen females — females which, if they were to be in such situations today, we would call slavery — the abandonment of which caused the majority of females to become males, as was what naturally occurred in the event of the death of the Ur-nadan, or the head male. This influx of male nadanians to NEC outposts, coupled with the simplex virus, was what allowed nadanians to interbreed with humanians, give birth to the namanians, and assist with the colonization of the rest of Nada, none of which would have happened if not for this series of events, no matter how unfortunate. The Universal Government has done everything in its power to improve the lives of both nadanians and namanians (and, for that matter, humanians, too), and, yes, not everything that the Universal Government did was, if looked at through the lens of current times, laudable, but today is not yesterday, and if we continue to wallow in the horrors of the past (a past which is hundreds of years behind us, for which reparation after reparation has been made), then we will never be able to move forward together. There will always be this sense of victimhood, aggressor and aggressee, oppressor and oppressed. We will continue to be stalled in every effort that seeks to treat one another as equals, for there is no difference in the nadanian from the humanian, or the namanian from the nadanian. We are equally capable, equally resilient, and we should be treated as such under the law. No thoughtful creature, be they human or alien, should have any more or any less rights than the other...

At which point there was a flurry of comments, messages and emails because Liam Melnykczuk had used the word 'alien', which, in his defense, and it was a defense which he voiced, he used because he was referring to nadanians as aliens under the alien act, which was also the subject of the book that they had all gathered together, at lunch, no less, to discuss. Further, the book itself used the term 'alien' when referring to Nada's original inhabitants, precisely for the same reason that Liam had. But his words were of little use – there was a hyper-sensitivity to any kind of criticism, no matter how slight, which, in Liam's mind, was not so much 'criticism' as it was 'providing an historic context,' a context that many, it had seemed, had forgotten, or, much more likely, had never taken the time to learn in the first place.

Without a doubt there were others who agreed with what Liam had been trying to express, but they stayed silent, which was what Liam should have done all along. It was nothing that Liam faulted them for. He understood their reasons quite well, even more so now that he was fired.

The incident reminded Liam of another episode, one that occurred well before the alien book club. The time he *did* stay silent; solemnly so, for, at the time, there was a sense of death – a death of reason, sanity, of shame, perhaps.

It occurred at the annual departmental meeting, a meeting which was hardly annual, but was one that Liam helped organize. He stood before a table covered with prizes which he had purchased with his own money. (The organizing committee had used all of its available funds renting a space large enough for all the staff.) Normally, staff were spread widely throughout Nada's constellations of asteroids, but the annual meeting required them to spend a significant amount of time traveling, jumping from asteroid to asteroid, to the head office at Rock Nippan to discuss ways in which they could improve operational efficiency, identify challenges/solutions, and otherwise just shoot-the-shit. All of this, Liam knew, took them away from their not insignificant amount of not undemanding work, labour for which they were, in Liam's opinion (because it applied to him just as much as it applied to them), underpaid. They were doing the duties of multiple full-time positions which remained unfilled and yet the work must still be done. The least Liam could do was reward them for, in their likely words, dealing with this kind of crap, and so he had bought, or found, an array of door prizes – books, chocolates, molerin-shaped wax candles, framed photographs, hand towels, beer koozies – trinkets that anyone could take simply for attending.

Liam stood before the prize table when Walter came up to stand beside him. Walter was a nadanian engagement officer and, given that he was nadanian himself, it was a role for which he seemed well-suited. Liam asked Walter what prize he was going to choose, and Walter replied, "Well, certainly not *that* one," pointing at one of the paintings that Liam, or, rather, Liam's wife, Jenn, had framed. It was amateurishly painted, with bright colours and poor shadowing, perhaps done for an art class, likely something that Jenn had found for pennies at a thrift store. It showed an ancient-looking spaceship, which Liam guessed was supposed to depict one of the original nadanian exploration company ships, landing on a yellow and purple asteroidal surface. Above it was the blobby inflorescence of a hovering giant sapseed. It was a simple, somewhat common painting, and Liam had seen many like it before.

As if Walter could see Liam's confusion, he tapped the painted sapseed and said: "This here, this represents nadanians. It represents *me*. And so, as a nadanian, when I see something like this," Walter poked at the NEC spaceship, "what I see is the colonization of my people, and it's very *triggering* seeing something like this. It's traumatizing. What this painting is showing is the continued *traumatization* of nadanians, because colonization is very *traumatizing*, you have to remember that, and it's *triggering* to look at. Like, when I see something like this all it does is remind me about how much our people have suffered, all of the pain that they were forced to carry over the generations. This painting is symbolic of all of that generational suffering, and so when I see this, as a nadanian, all I see is that pain, that suffering from colonization. It was forced on us, remember that."

Liam doubted that Walter's interpretation was what the artist, whoever they were, had originally intended. He thought the painting could equally represent the complete opposite: the resilience of nadanians, their perseverance in the face of colonial violence. He could point to the fact that the sapseed is painted over top of the spaceship, that it's opening, which could represent an overcoming of obstacles, victory over historic wrongs; he could have said that it represented the best of both worlds, the nadanian and the humanian coming together as one to create something that neither could create without the other - the collision of disparate pasts and the potential for a harmonious and united future. But Liam, knowing Walter, and knowing that Walter had an inordinate ability to go on and on and on in this kind of manner, said nothing, or, rather, said the following: "So chocolates, then?," which, as far as Liam was concerned, was much the same.

"Nonetheless," Walter continued, "Sometimes we have to be comfortable with being uncomfortable, because there are going to be a lot of hard discussions, and those discussions will be uncomfortable, and so we have to be comfortable being uncomfortable." It was something, in addition to his insistence that each and every meeting, no matter how small or unimportant, begin with an asteroidal acknowledgement, that Walter said often, in staff meetings, in the hallways, in public, 'we must be comfortable being uncomfortable', and whenever he did, it irked Liam. It was a sentiment that only ever went one way: that of the nadanian to the humanian. It was the humanian who must be comfortable in their discomfort, and never the nadanian; it was a sentiment that never went the other way, for if it did, as Walter had clearly interpreted the painting as implying, it triggered an avalanche of personal hurt and trauma, and that discomfort was to be avoided at all costs, or at least not displayed in a framed painting at the department's annual meeting, and, in all likelihood, no where else either.

Liam's phone rang, jolting him back into his body. It was Jenn. He took a sip of wine before answering.

"You messaged," she said.

"Yeah."

"And?"

"And you were right."

"Jesus Christ, Liam. I told you you shouldn't have said all of that."

"And you were right."

"So what are you going to do?"

"Right now I'm drinking wine."

"About your job."

"There's nothing I can do. Let it run through nadanian-humanian resources. Apparently there's a process. Maybe I can petition the director again later. I don't know exactly. Maybe there's nothing I can do. Maybe that's it."

"And in the meantime?"

"Vacation leave. Sick time."

"Which means."

"Well, I was thinking I'd go out to Rock Enor."

"Without me."

"You can certainly come."

"No. I mean, I can't, there's too much to do here, too much work. Besides, I told you I'm going to Rock Islin this weekend to see my parents."

"Ah, yes, sorry, I forgot."

"Are you sure you want to go to Seven Breezes? It's really early. I doubt anything's thawed. You'd have to take extra oxygen tanks."

"I thought I'd spend the rest of the day packing, then leave tomorrow. I have all the time in the world."

"Now?"

"Now, yeah."

"Jesus, Liam."

"There's nothing I can do about it now."

"You could have kept your mouth shut."

"I could have."

"Like the rest of us."

"But I didn't."

"And now you're fired."

"Technically, I'm *taking time for myself*."

"Message me before you leave."

"I will."

"And when you get to Seven Breezes."

"I will."

"Jesus, Liam."

"I know."

They hung up.

Liam finished the glass of wine.

Jenn, of course, was right. He shouldn't have said anything. He shouldn't have questioned the interminable nonsense about nadanian spirits inhabiting every nook and cranny, every splatfern and flea, every blackfish and spiner on Nada, despite the overwhelming evidence to the contrary. He shouldn't have said that all religions, even alien religions, are stupid. He shouldn't have questioned the self-important guest speakers when they belittled humanian science, which is not specifically humanian in nature, but rather a method meant to be universally applied, and instead emphasized the importance of other ways of knowing, which, as far as Liam could tell, included such ridiculous ideas as revelation through dreams. He shouldn't have reminded everyone that the process of science is one of minimizing bias, and that nadanian ways of knowing are not actually ways of discovering the truth, that the truth is hard to know and requires a concerted effort in which every attempt is made to reduce the influence of bias – bias which seems to be an integral component of nadanian science. And he certainly shouldn't have stood in front of a large gathering of nadanians, in his official capacity as a representative of the Universal Government for the purposes of court-mandated consultation with nadanians, who merely assert rather than provide concrete evidence that such-and-such an activity (quill harvesting, for instance) will have such-and-such impact on the practice of their treaty and nadanian rights. They instead surround themselves with a slew of lawyers and consultants, who are themselves predominantly not nadanian, and who use the court-mandated consultation process to extract public funds, because, of course, nadanian communities are not required to pay for the expenses themselves and instead rely completely on the Universal Government to foot the bill; to say nothing of the nadanian ahkeks and their well-compensated councillors, who not only encourage this kind of predatory behaviour on the part of lawyers and consultants, but actively benefit from it themselves, all at the expense of the people they are supposedly representing, who continue to live in untenable, unimaginable conditions where violence and drug and alcohol abuse goes wantonly unchecked. This seems to be the point of the entire nadanian-humanian relationship: poverty and abuse are wielded like swords to justify the perpetual transfer of hundreds of billions of dollars to a small, neotribal elite with no practical effect in remedying the problems the money is supposedly meant to solve.

But Liam Melnykczuk did say those things.

He stuffed another box of wine into his travel suitcase.

*Ryan Decision, 326PC.* Yther Ryan was convicted of hunting spiners on a private asteroid. He argued that it was a nadanian treaty right. Courts determined whether or not that right was extinguished by the asteroidal resources act. The court held that it had been extinguished.

# 2

Seven Breezes was officially registered as 2638314PC Rock Seven Breezes. It was a fifteen-minute jump from Rock Enor, which was itself a several-hour multi-jump from Rock Nippan. Liam Melnykczuk had made the trip many, many times before, usually with Jenn.

It was a 0.25 square kilometre asteroid on the edge of a large, blackly opaque inter-asteroidal cloudlake, pinched at the waist, almost as if a giant fist had gripped it when the rock was young and its exoskeleton was still malleable. Except for the clearing where a cottage was notched into the asteroid's northern end, much of the rock was covered in a dense, shaggy mat of quills, lesser sappers, splatfern, cone lice, and fungal and plant life typical of the asteroids that made up the Gar-Nada constellation.

It was a beautiful asteroid, and there were few things that Liam enjoyed more than simply walking under its canopy of feather quills, up and down its crags and long meandering footpaths, breathing in the rock's raw oxygen, which, in the summer, flowed from the ground like water. He loved listening to the indecipherable language of fleas, their clicks and grunts, the splash of crabs and blackfish as they swam and dove through the undulating waves of the cloudlake, and the ancient, prehistoric calls of the molerin. Although, ever since he first began accompanying Jenn to Seven Breezes, which was, in fact, her family's asteroid, he had heard their calls less and less. And when he did hear them, the molerin sounded rougher, thinner, somehow ailing compared to before. From what Liam could tell, the asteroid, especially its northern end, had once been a molerin breeding rock, and molerin, he knew, were fickle creatures who, like

Liam, preferred little else besides being left alone. Whether they had jumped to another asteroid in the region, one not notched with a cottage and landingway — and each year there were fewer and fewer of those kinds of asteroids — or whether they had simply died, Liam couldn't say. And now that he thought about it, he hadn't heard the call of the molerin for several years.

Liam lowered the small ship's passenger chair into its reclined position and turned on the radio. He had just passed the second lagrange point between Rocks Nippan and Enor, and would soon descend to make the final jump to Seven Breezes. The broadcaster's voice filled the ship's cabin.

"...is a foreign country, they do things differently there. But in light of the detection of possible unobserved burials at the former phrontistery dwelling at Rock Paradox, we have to ask ourselves if we have truly escaped our past, because if we don't confront our past, if we don't recognize that the past is not really behind us, then we'll never be able to..."

Liam turned it off. He had heard it all before; the narrative was everywhere, and he couldn't stand to listen to it any longer. How could someone detect something unobserved, possible or not? It was nonsense. That anyone could seriously entertain the idea that hundreds of nadanians would be surreptitiously buried, by other nadanians, no less, on orders of the phrontister heads, was ludicrous. That there could be possible unobserved burials could equally mean that they could be anything else: the refuse of wood-paneled outhouses, thousands of disintegrating nude photographs of the Universal Government's first minister, a midden of ratfruit pits that, lo and behold, look like nadanian hearts – the possibilities are endless because that is the nature of possibilities. That the Rock Paradox ahkeks glommed onto unobserved burials was completely without reason, and the claim that the possible unobserved burials represent the murdered bodies of young nadanians was being repeated ad nauseum, to the point that, yes, if one believed it, it *would* make one sick. In the media, on the radio, on television, on the internet, it was everywhere. And like many things that go viral, like rumours and ghost stories, hearsay and clickbaity tall-taling, it was not true. Not one of Nada's broadcasting corporation journalists, not one of the Universal Government's ministers, was challenging it, was asking for evidence, not one. It boggled the mind that everyone, nadanians and humanians alike, seemed quite willing to go along with what could only be described as self-flagellating bullshit. It was pure, unadulterated, concentrated bullshit. And, mused Liam, look what happened when one did call them out on their bullshit; they got fired, cancelled, you got labeled a specist in the media, a denier, or worse, a humanian fanatic. And it was bullshit, thought Liam, all of it, bullshit.

The ship whipped itself around, decelerated, landing gear out, and entered a long line of twenty, perhaps more, similar ships, whose passengers were all waiting to touch down on Rock Enor, refuel, and then jump onwards to Rock Bay, Rock Deception, Rock Red, or back to Rock Nippan. There were several thousands of asteroids to choose from, many of which were held by the Universal Government, but some, like Rock Seven Breezes, were private, and all were linked together by the intricate lagrange network system (prior to which many of Rock Enor's satellite asteroids remained inaccessible).

As his ship moved closer to the ground, Liam could see that both the lineup to land and the lineup to jump were longer than usual. Perhaps a crash, he thought. Rare, but not unheard of. Only once, in Liam's experience, was there a fatality: a freight ship had collided with a passenger ship, one very much like Liam's, killing its occupant; Jenn and him had been delayed for several hours at the Rock Enor transfer station while all the debris was collected.

And so, when Liam's ship finally did touch down, he was expecting, at worst, a tragedy, a collision, a fatality, perhaps, to be the cause of the delay, and even as the nadanian in green military fatigues approached, knocking on his ship's window as he did, Liam still thought it would be something of that nature. And, in a way, it was.

The nadanian knocked again, and Liam unsealed the door.

"Passing through?" said the nadanian, a large scar traced his face from the ear across the jawline and out toward his chin. Liam saw that there were others in fatigues around them, some had their heads bent into the doors of docked ships, much like the nadanian in his own door was doing. Some stood in authoritative postures, hands clasped, backs erect, motionless. No guns, or at least none that Liam could see, but there was a sense, in the slow turning of their heads, scanning from side to side, that if a gun was required, one would be produced. All were nadanian. All had, on their shoulders, the red warrior patch of ARM, the asteroidal reclamation movement – worn at protests, at rallies, at the parliament building in Rock Nippan; whenever and wherever ahkeks gathered, you'd see the image on over-sized red flags trailing their bearers like shadows, but one never saw them at a transfer station, and especially not the transfer station on Rock Enor. Or, at least, Liam hadn't.

"Passing through," he said again. It was no longer a question.

"Passing through, yeah. What's going on? Was there a crash?"

"A crash."

"Yeah."

"No crash, not yet."

"So what's going on then?"

"Where you jumping to?"

"What does it matter?"

"Well it does."

"To who?"

"To me."

"And who are you?"

"Where to?"

"Near here. Rock Seven Breezes."

The nadanian looked up, as if trying to see the asteroid somewhere in the dark sky.

"Never heard of it."

"How is that my problem? You have now."

"Have now."

"Heard of it, yeah."

"Seven Breezes."

"Yeah. Seven Breezes."

"Out that way?" He pointed in a direction.

"More or less."

"More or less."

"Yeah."

"Well which is it?"

"Which is what?"

"Is it more or is it less?"

"What?"

"Is it more or is it less?"

"More. Yeah, it's out that way."

"Thank you. Stay here."

The nadanian walked over to another in fatigues, spoke to him briefly, and then returned.

"It'll be thirty to jump to Rock... what do you call it?"

"Seven Breezes."

"Thirty to Seven Breezes."

"Thirty what?"

"Dollars."

"What?"

"Thirty dollars to jump to Rock Seven Breezes. You in a cottage, right? You'll be coming back, it don't look like you have a lot of O-tanks, you'll be coming back. So, thirty."

"Thirty for what?"

"Service fee. You're on nadanian land."

"I'm on nadanian land?"

"That's right. And you don't look nadanian."

"No, I'm not. Well..."

"Well what?"

"Technically, I'm namanian."

"You're a naman?"

"Technically."

"Technically?"

"Yeah."

"Well, prove it."

"What? How?"

"Let me see your hands."

"My hands?"

"Your hands."

Liam spread his fingers in front of him, and for a moment, they looked to him like they didn't belong, like ten prolapsed tubes of flesh and bone.

"I see ten fingers," said the nadanian.

"Well, yeah, and you'd be right."

"Nadanians have twelve. Same with namanians."

"Not all of them, they don't."

"Not all what?"

"Namanians. Look, I don't have the card, I don't have twelve fingers, but I am namanian. Technically."

"You don't look it."

"Do we ever?"

The nadanian laughed.

"What?"

"It's true is all. They don't ever look it. I mean, look at me."

Liam looked.

"I look nadanian. Put me in a lineup with humanians, and if you were told to pick the nadanian, you'd pick me, wouldn't you?"

"Yeah."

"And you'd be right. But you, you namanians, you all look like humanian. That's why I look at the hands."

"You said it's thirty to pass?"

"Fifteen, given you're a naman. Or so you say."

"I am. Technically."

"Look, I don't so much as care about that, but as far as I'm concerned, you're still on nadanian land, it's not namanian land, it's not your land, and it certainly isn't humanian, it don't belong to the Universal Government."

"When did you start?"

"Collecting?"

"Yeah, for the, uh, service fees, as you say."

"Just the other day. Council passed a new resolution, says this is our asteroid, says it's about time we start benefiting from it."

"Council did?"

"That's right."

"What council?"

"Rock Enor council."

"Interesting."

"Why's that?"

"Rock Enor council is established by the Universal Government. And you don't recognize the Universal Government."

"That's right."

"It's interesting is all."

"It don't change the fact that you're on nadanian land."

"How many are paying? The others you're stopping. All of them?"

"More or less." He smiled.

"You do realize this may be illegal."

"Not if it's nadanian land it isn't."

"And what's the service?"

"Protection."

"Protection?"

"That's right. We're land protectors."

"And the land needs protecting?"

"This land does."

Liam opened up the ship's console, removed his wallet, and counted out several bills.

"You said fifteen?"

"Fifteen."

"Here's a hundred. For the land. My wife may be coming along later. That should cover her as well. She's humanian, not namanian, if that matters."

"It does." The nadanian nodded, took the money, and tapped the door frame before pushing off and walking away.

***

When Liam landed at Seven Breezes, he saw that the cottage's glass and metal roof was covered in splatfern. He'd need to clear them off before they caused damage, before Jenn came. He unloaded the ship: food and water, clothes, the additional oxygen tanks he'd need to use, at least until the asteroid started to produce its own (which, given the season, may not be for quite a while). Most important of all, he unloaded the nadanian wine, in bulk.

He poured himself a glass and messaged Jenn that he'd arrived. It would be several hours before the signal reached her on Rock Islin.

*Pawani Decision, 326PC.* Danla Pawani was charged with selling cloud crab under a permit meant for food and ceremonial purposes. She argued it was her nadanian right to sell cloud crab commercially. The court ruled that the commercial sale of cloud crab was not integral to nadanian culture.

# 3

Liam Melnykczuk woke mid-morning to faint starlight, which traveled an expansive distance to reach the cloudlake only to be smothered by the lake's thick plumes, caught by photosynthetic rain eels, reflected away by the iridescent scales of blackfish, or eclipsed by other asteroids; despite it all, the starlight made it through, or at least some did, and, as spring turned into summer, more and more starlight would do so. It danced across Liam's face in shimmering patterns, thanks, in part, to the outstretched feathers of a copse of quills that stood sentinel outside the bedroom window. The cottage was cold, and Liam remembered he'd turned off the heat the night before. When he arrived, he'd maxed every thermostat: in his bedroom, in the kitchen, in the living- and washroom, in the smaller upstairs bedroom. He'd heard the electric hum of baseboard heaters, and the entire building had, over the course of the night, as he hauled and unpacked his supplies, over his roasted chicken dinner, honey-glazed carrots and mashed potatoes, with a red wine gravy, and with red wine itself, during the time in which he scanned the cottage's bookshelves looking for something to read, or the stack of old movies, VHS, DVDs, looking for something to watch, and finding nothing, the building had warmed to a sweltering degree; and so, before lying on the old, brown couch, putting on his noise-cancelling headphones and typing *asmr triggers no talking* into his phone, Liam turned most of the thermostats to low. Too low, he saw. He also saw that at some point in the night, he'd moved to the bedroom.

Liam pushed back the duvet and dressed, putting on the red Snuggie that Jenn got him for Christmas several years ago.

The domed cottage was roughly open concept, designed by Wilf, Jenn's father. A narrow hallway bisected it into quarters: the living room overlooked the shallows of the cloudlake, the kitchen's windows looked toward the asteroid's smaller south end (scrub land, for the most part; the quills there were smaller, thinner, and tangled in pickle vines and dense thickets of cutweed; in spring, hareberries would twist their way through the mass and Liam would eat them by the handful), and the bedroom/washroom/powerroom occupied the other half of the main floor. It remained unfinished: exposed drywall sheeting, streaks of white joint compound, disconnected dishwasher, inconsistent baseboard trim, light switches without faceplates, cabinets hung without doors, pencil-marks still visible on the floorboards; but, over the years, as Wilf picked away at it – the parquet flooring, the kitchen's crown molding, the washroom tiling, the shower, the plumbing, the sewage recycling system – the Seven Breezes cottage (which Wilf insisted on calling *the cloudhouse*) had become a wonderful and relaxing retreat; though it was, as it was intended to be, rustic. Liam filled the coffee maker and went to the powerroom while it brewed to check the oxygen levels. Everything seemed normal. He turned up the thermostat and climbed the stairs to the upper bedroom, where the curved skylight turned the darkness of space into an azure astral sea. It was covered in splatfern. They'd drift in from the cloudlake, looking like plump garbage bags, sometimes by the hundreds, and then, as if someone had stabbed holes in their sides, they would release a slurry of fermented waste. It was how they reproduced. The sludge that landed would form leaf-like fronds, slowly during the first season, and then rapidly once they established themselves. They would form small balloons with an oily, purplish-blue sheen which would inflate until they released, floating up and into the cloudlake, where they'd mature into the garbage bags that would make the same mess that, from below, Liam was staring at. He'd clear them off before their roots dissolved the glass. The coffee maker beeped and Liam went down. He poured himself a cup and sat at the kitchen table to drink it. He checked his phone for a message from Jenn. Nothing. He turned on the radio and twirled the dial to the Universal Government's broadcast, but all he heard was static. The signals were poor today, it seemed, which was nothing new; they were, much like the starlight that woke Liam, much like Liam himself, just as everybody was, vulnerable to the unpredictable whims of an unfeeling, uncaring, unknowing universe.

He went outside, into the copse of feather quills just beyond his bedroom's window, and pissed. The air was thin. Too thin to be out without an O-tank. He coughed. Urine spattered his foot. He wiped it on a hunk of moss before staggering back inside. He coughed again.

The previous season, in the twilight days of an asteroidal autumn, Liam had set up a series of trail cameras across Seven Breezes. To catch what? He didn't know, but they were on sale, so he bought, appropriately, he thought, seven of them. One for each breeze. What he'd like to catch on camera was a spiner, but he wasn't sure if there were any on the asteroid. Like splatfern, they could come from elsewhere, the cloud, other asteroids, but even so, Liam somewhat doubted their presence on Seven Breezes. He'd seen no signs: no tracks, no discarded spines, which, if a spiner were present, should be there. They were solitary animals. Nadanians hunted them for their new, supple spines, and they were generally quite smart. They knew how to avoid people, which, to Liam, was for the best, because they were also known to attack and, in very rare instances, kill.

But there was one place on the asteroid that, in Liam's mind, could reasonably belong to a spiner: the den on the north end, almost exactly opposite the cottage. Liam called it a den, but it could simply be a hole in the ground. Right beside it, almost as if it were protecting the site, loomed the slowly decaying corpse of a giant sapseed. It had been dead for as long as Liam had been coming to the cottage, and had likely died long before that. Nearly a meter wide at the base, its bole carried for fifteen, maybe twenty, meters into the air, where its top, the part that, if it had still been living, would have produced the sapseeds, had been snapped off; and yet, its ancient corpse remained. Liam called it the great spirit, and it was there that he had set up several trail cameras, from different angles, to capture whatever was in the den: a spiner, some unknown species, or, much more likely, nothing at all.

He ate eggs and toast for breakfast, clasped an O-mask around his skull, tactical boots, grabbed the buck knife, and, still draped in the red Snuggie, set out toward the den of the great spirit.

The trail led away from the cloudlake, up an incline, through a dense quill stand (knot and jelly quills mostly), none tall or wide enough for harvesting, give them another hundred years or so, thought Liam. As he hiked, he pushed aside any punchplants that hung from the lower quills and spotted an empty swat flea hive. The grey husk seemed to have a bite taken out of it; papery chunks flapped in the slight wind. Good, there was a wind, that meant the oxygen was returning.

When the trail ended, Liam continued to climb around a rock face painted with mature splatfern, their purple-blue flowers like puff balls at the end of long, filamentous stalks. He trudged through a patch of waist-high hiss nettles, which gave out no sound as he passed. A long carpeted stretch of canker moss brushed softly against his skin. Ahead was the den and the great spirit: the giant sapseed.

Over the years, Liam had walked through all of Seven Breezes, and, as far as he could tell, this was the only giant sapseed. There were the car-sized mounds of queen fleas that dotted the south end; there were the quill slugs that made porous middens at the base of nearly every quill; there were jam roots and pipe fingers and hareberries; but there were no other giant sapseeds, only one, and it was long dead.

Trail camera. Den. Giant sapseed. Everything was covered in a thin coating of quill hairs. The den appeared inactive. He saw a narrow quill slug trail, what appeared to be the footprints of a prawn fisher, and a lot of small black scat bear pellets. Liam downloaded the data from each camera and sat beside the den, leaning against the great spirit. He flipped through the images on his phone. Three hundred from each camera, each ingrained with data: date and time, temperature, oxygen levels. He looked through every photo for some disturbance –

the long claw of the spiner, its hairy legs, its luminescent eyes peering out from the darkness – he found nothing. The den, like the sapseed above it, was dead. He went to the other cameras and downloaded their data without checking what they contained.

On his way back to the cottage, he stopped to sit at a familiar rock, which at midday was awash in starlight. He would often stop at that rock, which he called the rainbow rock, and watch as the rainbow fleas emerged from their winter slumber. They were no larger than a fingernail, tapered at each end like a banana, head and fore-ends nearly indistinguishable, except for the dual pair of dull black eyes on one end. Their skin, a hard chitinous exoskeleton, the colour of an oil slick, hid two pairs of folded up wings. Every spring, for hours, Liam would silently sit and watch the colours bleed together in the starlight, swirling like cold cream in hot black coffee.

When it was cold and oxygen levels were low, as they were in the spring, rainbow fleas were slow, lethargic creatures, easily caught under one's cupped palm. Only in the summer were they agile enough to escape. Even so, Liam rarely saw them at any time other than early spring. In the summer, they spread themselves thin across the asteroid, but in the spring, tunneling out from the fibrous duff layer, they gathered by the thousands at rainbow rock, likely because its angle caught the star light like a solar panel.

Liam was careful to avoid accidentally stepping on any of them. He learned to sit still. It was remarkable how their colours camouflaged them against the mica and quartz and feldspar of the granite background; and the more he sat and watched, the more he saw, their slight movements exposing their presence.

Nestled in the duff, they entered a kind of hibernation, a diapause, slowing their metabolism to a standstill. Attracted by the imperceptible warmth of the starlight, they roused themselves awake. One of the first things they did was fuck, prioritized well above filling what must surely be their empty stomachs. That was what brought them to rainbow rock: their fuck pad, as Liam would crassly tell others. Liam loved to sit and watch.

He was mesmerized the first time he saw this spectacle, and, wanting to know more about rainbow fleas, read whatever literature he could find on them, which was surprisingly scant. Fred Hazelwood's highly cited tome on fleas mentioned they existed and described them based on a few specimens he observed in nature. He determined that they were widely distributed throughout Gar-Nada and were closely related to the smaller coal flea, but that was about it. And so, Liam looked toward the established biological understanding of spring fleas, of which both rainbow and coal fleas were members, and inferred from that their ecological role.

They were common and, as such, overlooked and undervalued. They were meant to be eaten, as many creatures were. They were tasteless, if a bit astringent, and not poisonous, as Liam personally discovered. They didn't pollinate quills or punchplants or hiss nettles; if anything, they were a nuisance, a pest.

Though not considered spring fleas, there were similar species that caused significant damage to harvestable quill stands. As diagrammed in Dr. Hazelwood's book, their long, cylindrical proboscises cut into quill boles, tonguing for sap, causing undesirable deformations: entire quill stands, typically tall and straight, turned into gnarled, haggard, low-lying bushes. Rainbow fleas very likely fed in a similar manner, although Liam had yet to see any kind of damage associated with it. They were, it seemed, generalists, gorging themselves on anything they could find.

But, while Liam observed, they were not concerned with feeding. Rather, their tiny brains were flooded with an array of chemicals that drove them to mate, which they did with an unabashed zeal.

Males, he saw, scurried around in short bursts, turned in half-circles, flitting their wings in a series of pulses, sometimes singly, as if they were trying to first get the attention of a female, and then, doubly, triply, up to eight wing clicks in quick succession, only to turn and around in the other direction, scurry away, or around the female, to do it again. Scurry turn click, scurry turn click, scurry turn click. It wasn't the most elaborate of mating displays, but the females, on whose attention this activity was focused, seemed entertained. They stood, motionless for the most part, and watched, turning to face the male when he circled around her, and sometimes clicking, always singly, in response. The dance wasn't always successful; Liam saw plenty of attempts where the scurry turn click dance was an embarrassing failure, and the female would not just scurry away but hop and fly away in rejection. But when it worked, when she was sufficiently impressed, the female wouldn't turn to face the male as he circled behind her; he'd click a few more times, as if testing her willingness, and then tentatively climb onto her back. There were times when, with a male on her back, the female clicked, as if she were trying to buck him off, and, sometimes, she did, whereupon the male would start, once again, at the beginning: scurry turn click, scurry turn click. But if she didn't buck him off, or if she didn't crawl under a quill feather in an attempt to pry him off, the pair would continue in that fashion for several minutes, and then the male would turn around, in a position that, Liam read, was called back-to-back copulation, and in that position they'd stay for several hours. Liam knew this to be the case because, in his fascination, he collected several mated pairs and, in an old aquarium, separated each pair into their own little chamber, their own little fuck pad, and timed them. One pair maintained that position for eighteen hours. He released them afterward.

In their exuberant pheromonal glee to mate, male rainbow fleas would sometimes bound upon the backs of other males. Presumably, these were cases of mistaken identity and not some flea-based homosexual proclivity. At one time, Liam observed not just one, but three males simultaneously engaged in this way.

Coal fleas, though not as numerous as the rainbow fleas, also gathered at the rainbow rock to fuck.

But mistaken identities, it seemed, breached the species divide. Not infrequently, Liam saw male rainbow fleas attempting to mate with female coal fleas; although several of them could well have been male coal fleas, and so the observation could represent an example of inter-species homosexuality, which, if it were the case, had not been described in the scientific literature; in this way, Liam was a pioneer.

And so, Liam sat on rainbow rock in his red Snuggie and watched as thousands of rainbow fleas scurried and turned and clicked, popping like stovetop popcorn all around him until the starlight begun to fade. He then walked back down the winding trail, around the punchplants, through the knot and jelly quills, and back to the cottage.

He poured himself a glass of wine, ate some cold chicken, and checked the images from the other cameras. Nothing but quill slugs and scat bears. He turned on the radio, expecting static, but the voice of one of Rock Enor's broadcasters came through clearly:

"...Chloe Troughburn, minister of parliament for Rock Nippan, has introduced a bill to amend the criminal code of Nada to, she said at a press conference this afternoon, include the willful promotion of hate against nadanians by condoning, down-playing, or justifying the phrontistery dwellings.

"'It was genocide, pure and simple. And I want to thank the nadanian survivors, first and foremost, because this is about them. And this bill will protect them from violence, further violence, further incitement of hate, of hate crimes, after enduring what happened at the phrontistery dwellings, and, after what we saw at Rock Paradox, this bill is even more important, and that's what this bill to amend the criminal code will do, prevent the...'".

The static returned. Liam looked for a message from Jenn and saw none. He put on his headphones, typed in *asmr cranial nerve roleplay*, and clicked the first video that came up; a blonde humanian welcomed him into her office. He took another sip of wine, laid down on the couch, and closed his eyes.

The doctor would see him now, and he fell asleep.

*Perry Decision, 326PC. Rock Perry community members were charged with selling more molerin eggs than their licence allowed. They were caught selling 2,000 kilograms when their licence allowed for only 150 kilograms. The members argued they had a nadanian right to commercially exploit molerin. The courts ruled that although molerin eggs were traded prior to humanian contact, it wasn't done for commercial purposes; therefore, nadanian rights were not exclusive to others' rights.*

# 4

Liam woke to a knock at the door, still on the couch, still in the red Snuggie. He sat up and listened, tearing off the headphones by the cord, squinting, as if his eyes were new and needed to be worked in. The knocking continued as he went to the door.

On the other side was Merlan Mykhailuk, from across the cloudlake. Liam looked out the window and saw Merlan's single-seater tied up on the shore; it was good for short-distance jumping, catching cloud crabs and blackfish, scouting around asteroids, but not much else. Off-grid, disconnected from the lagrange network, it was easy to get stranded in if the winds weren't going your way, or the engine failed. Liam was fairly sure there was one in storage, tucked under the cottage, but he'd never used it. Merlan frequently used his.

He was a large man, taller than he was wide, but not by much, and missing two fingers on his left hand; he'd had, from what Liam could tell, every job in the world (including boxer and bouncer, debt collector, and, probably, mercenary). Fortunately for Liam, Merlan liked him.

"M'boy!" he said as Liam opened the door. "Wilf said you were here."

"Wilf?"

"When I saw the ship docked, I thought it was him, so I called, but he said it was you who was out here, so now I'm paying a visit. Just came from the Seidelskyys."

"The Seidelskyys are out?"

"Move aside."

Liam led him to the kitchen table. Merlan eased himself into one of the chairs, draping his thick coat onto its back. Liam heated up yesterday's coffee in the microwave.

"You okay?" said Liam.

"Age is all, m'boy, it'll come for you, too, don't worry. My leg, it doesn't quite move like it used to."

"Does it hurt?"

"Of course it hurts, everything does, you'll see one day."

"You said you talked to Wilf, did he say if Jenn was there? I haven't been getting a signal."

"It's off and on, but, ya, Jenn's there. That girl is a queen, you know."

"I know."

"A *queen*."

"What did Wilf say?" Liam poured into another cup. "Coffee?"

"Yeah, yeah. Said the blockade was extortion, and he's damn right about that, you know. They got no right to do what they're doing, I don't care what any council says, and I told them as much."

"You got through."

"I'm here, aren't I? I told the bastards that I ain't paying a damn cent. Wilf said you better not have paid them."

"I bargained them down. I told them I was namanian."

Merlan laughed.

"So did I, m'boy!"

"Are you?"

"Fuck, I better not be. I held up my hands like *this,* and I said 'you want to count 'em, well then count 'em.' And the bastard let me go. And that was the right decision they made, 'cause by then my fists were balls and I went like *this*." Merlan posed with his hands clenched. "You have anything stronger?"

"Like coffee?"

"Like booze, m'boy, like whiskey, anything."

Liam looked at the microwave.

"It's 8:15, Merlan."

"That's right, m'boy, I'm behind schedule. Plus, it'll help out the leg."

Liam went to the pantry, found a half-drunk bottle of crown royal and a shot glass, and placed the two on the table. Merlan filled the glass, drank it, then filled it again.

"Join me," he said. "I heard you got reason to be drinking."

"Reason?"

"Wilf said you got fired."

"Well, technically, I'm on vacation."

Merlan waved away the technicality as he sipped.

"Yeah, yeah – Wilf said you'd say that."

"And what did he say?"

"Just that it's a shame."

"Well it is."

"You said you're namanian?"

"My dad's mom's mom was nadanian, she lived way out in Rock Splitfoot, so yeah. I never knew her, but I'm told she died when she was nearly a hundred."

"And that's not enough to keep you from being fired?"

Liam filled his own shot glass and drank half. "Apparently not."

"Goddamn aliens."

Liam drank the rest. Merlan did too.

"It's just odd," Liam said. "I know a lot of atheists, or, at least, I know a lot of people who are practically, if not theoretically, atheists." He felt the whiskey hit him. "But what I've never seen, well, one maybe, but aside from that, I've never seen a nadanian atheist. They're either christian (catholic for the most part, but there's a weird mix of protestantism in there, too), or they're spiritualists, traditionalists or whatever. I never see nadanian atheists. Surely they must exist, but I don't know. You ask them if they believe in god, they say yeah, they believe in god, or spirits, or the great sapper, or something about the six directions, or the *first one*; that asteroids are living, breathing beings; that all life is temporary and that when you die your spirit will travel back and meld with the great sapper in the sky; that a soul enters the heart in the womb and forgets who it is upon birth, only the sap – the blood – can remember. The number six comes up often: it's always six this and six that, so there's definitely a deference for numerology; and then there's their belief in saparians and hars, which they call the spine people and who they think evolved from spiners, it's like their version of bigfoot or the loch ness monster or mothman, it's a fairy tale is what it is, and what are we supposed to do when someone thinks that burning sap crystals cleans the air and cures cancer? We're just supposed to go along with it? We're not allowed to say: No, that's not how things actually work? A lot of them think that the great sapper placed them directly on the asteroids, when we know, from genomic and archeological remains, that they came from Ur-Nada. Granted, yes, it was thousands of years ago, but that's quite a different thing from what they claim. Plus, some only arrived a couple hundred years before contact. Is that time immemorial? My point is, where are the atheists? Where is the skepticism? And a lot of this stuff, the *six ways* stuff, the stuff about the great sapper being the mother of us all, a lot of it isn't even traditional, it's new, imported from christianity, from humanian myths and legends, only given a nadanian twist; trauma is the new sin, it's inherited, and only healing ceremonies can bring about salvation. It's just nadanian new age garbage, no different from naturopaths or creationists or chiropracty or reiki or chakras or seeing auras – I mean, rivers of crap never flowed so thick."

"And that's what got you fired, is it?"

"More or less." Liam paused, then said: "More," and refilled both shot glasses.

"Well, I got something for you then, m'boy, and I think you'll like it 'cause there's parts in it about what you've been saying." And Merlan bent to his side, dug into a coat pocket, and removed a book. "Here you go. For being fired."

*The Survival Handbook: How to survive in the wild, in any climate, on any asteroid.*

"And look here," said Merlan, flipping to a page, tapping on it. "Right there."

Liam looked. In the introduction there was a section describing saparians, the nadanian elves.

"Isn't that what you were talking about? Well, there you go, m'boy, you're welcome."

"You don't believe in this, do you?"

"It's a nice story is all."

Liam sipped and nodded.

"I'll tell you a story, you'll see. It's about my grandfather. Now, my grandfather was always looking for women, you see, and each day when I was a little kid, he would take me to school along the river. This was in Rock Nippan. And one time as we walked, he stopped, and he shielded his eyes and looked up at the cloud above. And so I asked him, I said, Grandfather, what are you looking for? And my grandfather replied, Cloud women. Well, after school, he was there again, and we'd walk back home along the river. And as we walked, he looked at the ground as if he'd lost a coin or something in the dirt. So I said to him again, Grandfather, what are you looking for now? And he replied, Ground women. How many kinds of women are there, Grandfather? I asked. Many, m'boy, he said. There are grass women and rock women and cloud and ground women. And what kind of women are the best? I asked him. And he looked at the river and said, River women. River women are the best. Your grandmother was a river woman. When I first saw her, she was on the rocks where the river bends toward the bridge. This was before there was a bridge. Later, at dinner, I asked him, Grandfather, can I take your cloudboat to the bend in the river and look for women? And he said, No, I need my cloudboat for crabbing. But that evening, he didn't go crabbing. On the weekend, I didn't have school, and I found him sleeping, so I nudged him and asked, Grandfather, now that you're sleeping, can I take your cloudboat and look for river women? No, he said, I need my cloudboat for traveling. But then all weekend, I saw he didn't go traveling. So, one night, after grandfather had gone to sleep, I crept out of the house and went down to the river. I found his cloudboat on the bank with a short rope securing it. So I untied it, pulled it into the river, and went out toward the bend near the bridge. On the way, I went through a patch of grass, so I looked for grass women among their blades, but I didn't see any grass women. I passed near a cloud quill that bent itself over the river, so I looked for quill women in its feathers, but I didn't see any quill women. I looked at the stars, and I only saw the stars. I looked at the night, and I only saw the night. I looked at the cloud, and I only saw the cloud. No matter, I thought, Grandfather said that river women were the best. So I putted along in the cloudboat to the bend near the bridge where he said the river women would be. But when I reached the bend, I saw no women. I went up and around the bend, but I saw no women there either. I went downstream again, this time slowly, making sure I looked well and good over every rock, but I saw no women. I slapped the side of the cloudboat and was about to go home when I saw a small cloudboat, smaller than mine, carrying two hairless saparians, one at the fore and one at the rear of it, and they were boating over to the rocks where grandfather said the river women would be. Aha, I thought, maybe the saparians are looking for women, too! So I went along as quietly as the cloudboat allowed. I couldn't get too close or else the saparians may get upset, and then maybe they'd sink grandfather's cloudboat. Hidden at a distance, I watched as the saparians turned their cloudboat towards the rocks, but instead of slowing down, they went fast, faster than I thought a cloudboat should go. They were going so fast I was sure they'd end up in a crash, but then just as the tip of their cloudboat was about to touch the rocks, a crack formed, and the rock opened for the saparians just as a door would have done. A bright light, brighter than the stars, shone from within, and the saparians disappeared inside that light. Well, that must be where the river women were, I thought, and so I swung the cloudboat around and went as fast as I could toward the rocks where the saparians had gone. I could still see the bright light shining from the door. And then, *wham*! Instead of passing through as the saparians did, my grandfather's cloudboat crashed against the rocks. And then I must have hit my head on one of them because when I woke, it was nearly dawn. I could see the stars' hair peeking over the horizon. Oh no, I thought, grandfather would soon be awake! And when I looked at his cloudboat, I saw that there was a small hole in the front where it slammed against the rocks, so I wadded up one of my socks to plug the hole as best I could, and I went faster than hell to get back to the house before grandfather noticed where I'd gone and what I'd done. I passed by the cloud quill that held no quill women. I passed by the patch of grass behind whose blades hid no grass women. I passed under the clouds where no cloud women swam. I hadn't seen a single woman the whole night. When I finally arrived back at the house, I could see that grandfather was sitting at the kitchen table, and so I retied his cloudboat and crept around the back and through the window and into my room. I came out pretending I'd been sleeping the whole time, and grandfather said, Good morning, m'boy, I saw another kind of woman last night: a dream woman! She gave me a dirty wet sock. I wonder what that means. Dreams always have meanings, you know. And then grandfather looked at my feet, and I looked down at them too, and I saw that my right foot was bare. Where's your other sock, he asked, and I said, Well, it must have been the saparians have taken it, Grandfather. Oh yes, he said, the saparians will do that. They like playing tricks on people like that. I guess my dream woman found your sock! And he laughed and laughed and laughed about that, and, you know, he never did say anything about the hole I'd made in his cloudboat."

Merlan stopped, drank the full shot glass, and then said, "That's a nice story, isn't it?"

"But is it true?"

"Hell no, it isn't true. I made it up. My point is that stories don't have to be true to contain something true."

"So what's true about that story then?"

"That dream women exist, m'boy."

"Dream women."

Merlan pushed himself up, favouring his leg, and put on his coat. "You tell that dream woman of yours I said hello, okay. Tell her she's the queen of all of Gar-Nada."

"I will."

"And whatever you got to do to get yourself unfired, you do that, too."

"You need me to help you to the boat?"

"I got it, I got it, I'm not dead yet, am I?"

Merlan limped down to the shore, started his single-seater, and launched himself back into the cloudlake. Blackfish shimmered in his wake.

Liam took the book from the table, slumped back on the couch, and opened it. It was written by a humanian soldier from Nada's armed forces.

*Accidents don't often announce themselves,* it read, *but when they arrive, you must be prepared. Your survival depends on it. Water, food, fire, and shelter – these are your basic needs, and, if you are prepared, only in rare cases would they be lacking in the environment; from the tops of frozen asteroidal mountains to their wet marshy valleys, from brilliant cloudlakes to interstellar deserts and everything in between, these basic needs are ready to be exploited, if you know how. But this handbook is only a guide; it cannot tell you what risks you will need to weigh in order to survive, but it will help you identify where those risks lie.*

Liam flipped to the page Merlan said: *The Giant Sapseed.*

Native to Ur-Nada, the giant sapseed was integral to the early colonization of Nada's constellations of asteroids. Without them, it is hard to imagine how they would have survived the harsh conditions of inter-asteroidal space, which is why the giant sapseed has been incorporated into many aspects of their culture. It provided their food, their clothing, and their transportation. Young saproots, though pliable when fresh, could be dried into tubular straws, sap-pipes, or deadly spears. The sap is fragrant and highly nutritious and crystallizes into a waxy substance, which can be smoked or used as an incense. The structural filaments of its bole can be separated into thin ropes, perfect for snares or netting, or can be woven into blankets to protect against solar radiation. The discarded husks of expended shells provide the simple, domed shelter that nadanians are well-known for. And, of course, it was the sapseeds themselves that provided ancient nadanians with the vehicle and ability to jump from one asteroid to another: pressure, built up within the ripening sapseed, provides the necessary thrust to escape an asteroid's gravitational pull, allowing one to *ride the seed*; a phrase which has also come to mean *to leave*, *to ramble*, *to wander*, *to look for better days*, or *toward the future*. In many nadanian cultures, it also means *to die*, as it was a common practice to send the old or infirm, the sick, or, if resources proved unexpectedly scarce, the very young, to *ride the seed*.

There are also many myths and stories where the giant sapseed is central. For example, when the great sapper, sometimes called the first one, created all of Nada's asteroids, the first two nadanians, the hars, came from the first sapseed. When it split in two, one half of the shell became Ahmek, the good one, the trickster, who would, in other stories, create the saparians, and the other half became the bad one, the devil-like Ahmem.

The next several pages told the story of the great sapper.

When the great sapper first lived, the saparians did not know how to tame Ahmem, and he would go wherever he pleased and do whatever he pleased. If Ahmem wanted to roam beneath the quills, he would roam beneath the quills; if he wanted to climb to the top of a mountain, he would climb to the top of the mountain; and wherever he went, he would eat the saparians who lived there.

One day, when Ahmem was walking near a river, a river saparian saw him and swam up to the banks and said to him, Ahmem, where are you going? Without stopping, Ahmem said, I'm going over to the quills to eat the quill saparians that live there. So the river saparian swam upstream to where the quills were and yelled to the quill saparians, You better get down from those quills, Ahmem is coming! And he intends to eat you! But the quill saparians didn't come down from the quills. And when Ahmem came to where the quills were, he opened his mouth and shook all the quills so that the quill saparians fell inside.

The next day, Ahmem was again walking near the river, so a river saparian swam up to him and said, Ahmem, where are you going now? And without stopping, Ahmem said, I'm going to the mountains to eat all the mountain saparians who live there. So the river saparian swam as high as he could up the mountainside and yelled, You better get down from that mountaintop, Ahmem is coming! And he intends to eat you! But the mountain saparians didn't come down from the mountaintop, and when Ahmem arrived, he called up an avalanche, opened his mouth, and all the mountain saparians rolled down with it and into his gaping jaw.

This is no good, said Ahmem, opening and closing his mouth. I've got quill saparians stuck in my teeth like slivers, and the mountain saparians have coated my throat like sand. I know! I should eat the river saparians! That will help clean out the slivers in my teeth and that sand in my throat! So Ahmem went down to the river to eat the saparians who lived there. But the river saparian had seen Ahmem eat both the quill and mountain saparians and had heard him complaining, and so he went back to its ahket to warn them.

The saparian went to the oldest of their ahket and asked what they should do, and the oldest one gathered up all the river saparians and said to them, Saparians, today I must sacrifice my life to save yours. I will give myself up to Ahmem, who will surely recognize my valour and bravery, and because of this, he will respect my wish to let you all live. And then, when Ahmem arrived at the river's bank, the oldest one threw himself at him and was quickly eaten. Yet Ahmem continued, and he climbed into the river.

Another saparian came forward, and this one was a well-respected ahkek, and he said, Saparians, today I must sacrifice my life to save yours. The oldest one was too skinny for Ahmem, while I am very fat. Ahmem will see this and be humbled that we have given him the fattest saparian among us, and so he will leave the rest of you alone. And he swam up to Ahmem and was quickly eaten. Yet Ahmem continued to walk deeper into the river.

Finally, after much deliberation, one saparian, who was neither too skinny nor too fat, said to all the others, Saparians, listen to me! Ahmem can do whatever he wants whenever he wants. We must accept that, eventually, each of us will be similarly eaten. And so why wait, we should all throw ourselves into his mouth, for he will eat us anyway, whether we like it or not. And so all the river saparians threw themselves at Ahmem, and soon his stomach was full of river saparians.

No, no, no, said Ahmem, burping. I am too full! I cannot eat you all at once! Please, each one of you wait your turn! But the saparians continued to throw themselves into Ahmem's open mouth.

This is too much! complained Ahmem. I must rest before I eat another. Just looking at you makes me want to puke. And so Ahmem pulled himself to shore and went to sleep.

It's a good thing he was so full, said one of the surviving saparians. There aren't many of us left.

Don't worry, said another. As long as Ahmem is full, he will continue to sleep. All we have to do is keep him full.

But what will we feed him? There are no more quill saparians living in the quills, and there are no more mountain saparians living on the mountain.

I know, said one. While we were fleeing Ahmem, the nadanians went to live in the quills because there were no more quill saparians. And while we were throwing ourselves at Ahmem, the nadanians went to live on the mountain because there were no more mountain saparians there either. We will feed Ahmem the nadanians!

So when Ahmem began to wake, the river saparians went to the quills, grabbed a nadanian, and threw him into Ahmem's mouth. But it only helped a little. So they went to the mountaintop, grabbed another nadanian, and threw her into Ahmem's mouth. But it, too, only helped a little.

Throw in another! yelled one saparian.

It's working! Throw in more! yelled a second.

It's a good thing there are so many nadanians living in the quills and on the mountains, said a third.

And from then on, whenever Ahmem stirred as if to wake, the saparians would grab another nadanian and throw them into his open mouth.

And that is how the saparians learned to tame Ahmem.

Liam put down the book. His head swirled, as did the whiskey in his stomach. He looked at his phone, saw there was signal, and messaged Jenn about Merlan. He put on his headphones, typed in *asmr aggressive spit painting*, fell back on the couch and closed his eyes.

A whisper woke him.

*Liam.*

He was outside. Surrounded by quills. Another language, maybe. Nadanian. Pluck. He looked down and saw he was without his boots, only one foot covered by a sock. His mask. He looked for an extra tank in his pockets, but they were empty. He'd forgotten it at the cottage. The cottage. He looked to where it should be, but it wasn't there. Only quills. Empty ground. Pluck. Whispers. He followed a path around a rock outcrop. He pushed through a thicket of hiss nettles. They whispered, too. Down the path. To the den. The hole was dark, and Liam could tell there was something inside. Too dark. But that's where the whispers came from. *Hello.* Pluck. Liam heard it licking its lips. Eating something. Crunching it between its teeth. *Hello, my lovely.* Closer. Liam was on his knees. *You're safe here.* The darkness in the hole expanded, as if breathing. In. *Hello.* Out. Pluck. It swallowed something. *My lovely.* A tongue flicking aside sinew. Liam put his head inside. *Hello.* Fat sucked off the bone. Deeper. *Shhhh, it's okay. You're safe now, my lovely.* Closer. *You're doing such a good job.* White eyes opened. An animal's. A spiner's. Ahmem's. *I'm so proud of you.* They lunged, and Liam fell backward. He was looking at the sky, deep azure, filled with blackfish. A thin, clawed leg retreated into the den, scraping the rock and dirt. Scratching. *Three.* The bole of the giant sapseed stabbed upward. Its skin peeled in strips. Narrowed. *Two.* Liam's gaze followed it up. Above him. Towering. Not broken. Not here. It continued into the sky. Bare skin. A waist.

A belly button. Up and up and up. Ribs. Nipples. Breasts where sapseeds would be. They grew. Ripened. Cleaved off and floated up. *One.* And up and up. Into the blackfish sea. Shoulders. *You're doing so good.* A neck. A head. A face. Jenn's.

*And stop.*

Liam woke up on the couch, ripped out of the dream by an ad for razor blades. Too much whiskey, he thought. And the dream woman faded.

*Untiban Nation Decision, 327PC.* Untiban Nation members claimed that 5,000 asteroids should be under their jurisdiction, arguing they had title. While their claims were dismissed, it established that for nadanian title to exist, they must show they once occupied the asteroid, continue to occupy the asteroid, and that occupation must be exclusively theirs.

# 5

Liam sat at the kitchen table, drank his coffee, and flipped through the survival handbook.

*Begin by preparing yourself to be a survivor. A knife is your most important survival tool. Always carry one. Always keep it in perfect condition.*

Liam found his buck knife, a ten-centimeter stainless steel folding DeWalt, partially-serrated blade with a wire stripper. He unfolded it, ran his finger over its edge, refolded it, and placed it in the large front pouch of his Snuggie.

He turned pages, scanning the book's contents: How to Find Water and Create a Solar Still. How to Protect Yourself if Your Ship Crash Lands. How to Make a Fire. How To Know if a Plant or Fungus is Poisonous or Edible.

He stopped at the section on dens.

*Many animals make their homes in dens, usually on high ground away from water. Some, such as scat bears and quill slugs, take little trouble to conceal them, although one or two exits will be hidden for use in an emergency. Scat bears' emergency holes are easily dug out. Barbed wire or the stem of a ratfruit can be pushed down the hole to hook the scat bear out. Predatory animals are known to hide their holes, which are generally found in quilled areas. Tracks or droppings nearby may give their location away and are an indication that a hole is in use.*

He continued to read. How to Make a Simple Snare. A Baited Spring Leg Snare. A Double-Ended Figure Four Snare. A Square-Face Release Trap. A Bow Trap.

A Hole Noose. Weapons. Slings. Bolas. Spears. How to Trap Cloud Crabs and Blackfish. How to Create a Gill Net. Weirs. Quill Shelters. Walls and Screens. Lean-Tos. Tongs and Pot Rods. Spoons and Knot Quill Containers. Stone and Bone Tools. How to Fix a Broken Axe Handle. Tube Beds and Travoises. How to Make Rope From Hiss Nettles. The Crabber Knot. The Clove Hitch. How to Read a Cloudlake. How to Predict the Weather. How to Navigate by the Stars. How to Prevent Gangrene Using Gun Powder.

Liam leaned back into his chair. Much of the 640-page handbook wouldn't apply to an asteroid like Seven Breezes. He'd start with something small, he thought, something easy, and chose the Bottle Trap.

*If you have a plastic bottle, you can make an efficient trap for small blackfish by cutting it off just below the neck and then inverting the neck inside the bottle. Smaller blackfish will swim in but will not be able to find their way out again. Bait the trap to entice them in.*

There was a diagram illustrating its construction.

Liam went into the fridge, poured a bottle of water out into a pitcher, cut off a hunk of chicken, wrapped it in cellophane, and put both into the Snuggie's pouch with the knife. He grabbed the book, a roll of fishing line, and his oxygen mask. He went outside to the cloudlake's shoreline and emptied everything onto the ground.

He stabbed the plastic bottle, cut out the top, inverted it, pushed tightly to secure it inside. Twirling the blade's tip, he made a hole in the side and ran the line through. He added the bait and unhooked his mask and pulsed a bit of oxygen inside to give it lift.

The bottle trap floated up into the cloudlake and Liam let out about twenty-five metres of line, cut it, and tied the end to a rock as an anchor.

He watched the bottle for several minutes. Watched the cloudlake's plumes ebb, shifting from translucent to opaque and back again. It was hypnotic. Relaxing.

Liam stood there, transfixed by its impermanence, by the bottle trap bobbing, by the odd solace it provided.

A light wind turned the cloudlake over and his focus slid to the building behind it. The Seidelskyys'. It was a large place, domed much like the Seven Breezes cottage, but three stories instead of two. Their ship was there, and a large lawn, likely of carpet moss, stretched down to the shore. Someone was walking back from a small storage shed near the shore's edge.

Liam went back to the cottage, emptied several more water bottles into the pitcher, and returned.

He looked to the ground for his knife. There was the fishing line, the wad of chicken bait, the book – but no knife. He patted his pouch and pockets. Nothing. He walked to where he'd anchored the line to the rock. Still nothing. He walked back up the path to the cottage and back again in case he'd dropped it, but it wasn't there either. He'd lost the knife, a survivor's most important tool.

He went back to the cottage and looked around inside for another one. He rummaged around the closet in the upstairs bedroom. There were boardgames, Wilf's clothing, boxes of parquet tiling, multiple tape measures, a telescope, a FosPower solar crank portable radio, a gun case, but no knives. He went back downstairs, into the kitchen's utensil drawer and took out a chef's knife. He went back to the shore where he'd left the emptied plastic water bottles and began to cut. The bottle folded into the knife, crumpling, and when Liam applied more pressure the cut sliced at an angle, ruining it.

Liam looked up at the bottle trap he'd made. One would have to do. He gathered the line and book and bait and went back inside. He poured himself a glass of wine and looked out across the cloud, toward the Seidelskyys'. He could see something on the lawn, a speck among the carpet moss. He went upstairs, grabbed the telescope, and looked through the finderscope to get a closer look.

The speck was a young woman, the Seidelskyy's daughter, and she was naked, suntanning herself on a black patio-style chaise longue chair. Liam adjusted the focuser, looked through the eyepiece, switched it out for the larger one, and then looked again. She lay on her back, nearly flat, the chaise longue fully extended, her arms draped over its sides. Her hair looked to be dark blonde, roughly braided in two, each braid traced her neck and fell onto a bare shoulder; two curled blonde tendrils trickled down her face and hung by her scarlet lips, just below her small nose. Her chest pushed out over the terracing of her ribs. Her belly button was a small dark dip on the light desert of her stomach. If Liam held still he could see the small drops of perspiration, small oases, that dripped down into the shadows of her crossed legs. The soles of her narrow feet were peppered with flecks of moss.

Liam watched her for some time. She leaned up on her elbows and turned to reach for a glass of something, and when she did Liam saw the fullness of her breasts. He watched her throat muscles constrict as she swallowed the liquid. She flipped onto her stomach and bent forward and arched her slim back to stretch.

At times the cloudlake would blow in and obscure her, and Liam would take the opportunity to refill his wine glass, but for the much of the afternoon, it was, luckily for him, a bright and clear day.

Eventually, she sat up, finished her drink, and removed her sunglasses. That's when an odd sense of familiarity struck Liam. He'd seen the Seidelskyy's daughter before. But where? Had they visited Seven Breezes at one time? Long ago? If so, she wouldn't have been much more than a girl at the time, and that's not what caused Liam to pause. He put the smaller eyepiece back in and steadied it on her face. Her blue eyes. The faint trace of winged eyeliner. In this new light, her hair and eyebrows could be a strawberry blonde.

And then it hit him. Autonomous Sensory Meridian Response. She did ASMR. Liam scrolled through his phone's search history. *Three hours of ear eating. Goth girl does your make-up. Nerdy librarian helps you study. Asmr towel folding tutorial*. Hundreds of videos flew by. He typed in *asmr Seidelskyy* knowing nothing would come up. He typed in *asmr full body examination* and *asmr lotion sounds* and, in a desperate attempt, *asmr big tits*. Nothing. No hits.

It was only when he typed in *asmr mic pumping on knees* that he found it. Her name – her ASMR name – was Dolly Lilith. He clicked on her profile and then opened a video titled *ASMR Long SMASHING BUBBLE WRAP Good for Relaxation* and watched. In the video, her hair was pulled back into pigtails and she wore a white wide-necked crop top over a bright pink lace bra, her stomach bared, and she sat on a bed popping bubble wrap between her long, painted nails. The sounds of plastic, like saran wrap, filled Liam's headphones. On her chest, just above the fine line of her cleavage, was a series of birthmarks, strawberry marks, really, in a small triangle that pointed down.

Still listening to the video, Liam returned to the telescope. Dolly was once again lying on her back, and there, slightly above and between her naked breasts, caught between the rouge of her prim nipples, was the triangle. It was her. Dolly Lilith Seidelskyy.

Liam listened to several other videos as he watched. *Dolly Lilith ASMR – Mouth sounds, chewing, and gentle tapping. Dolly Lilith ASMR – Relaxation, mic pumping, and whispers. Dolly Lilith ASMR – Pleasure sounds and intimate touching.* He clicked a link on one of the video descriptions and it took him to her OnlyFans page. He signed up, adding his address and credit card information, and subscribed to her page for $9.99 a month, unlocking her profile.

Hundreds of images of her flooded his feed. In lingerie. In swimsuits. In nothing at all. He clicked on a video and she began to whisper to Liam. She played with the fabric on her top, traced her fingers up and down its spaghetti straps, pulled it out and let it snap against her skin and against the thinly-veiled roundness of her nipples. She cupped her breasts and roughly fluttered her hands over them, she bent forward and breathed into the mic, she sighed, she made muffled chirp noises and clicked her tongue, she moaned. And it was, despite its clearly stimulating intent, deeply relaxing. As if it were one of her fingernails, Liam felt a warm, tingling sensation trace itself down his neck and spine.

On the other side of the cloudlake, Dolly Lilith had gone inside, and so Liam sat on the couch, clicked on another video, and watched.

"Hello, my lovely," she whispered. "I hope you experience a lot of tingles, a lot of pleasure, to relax your whole body."

Dolly sat on the edge of a sofa bed covered in a pink shag blanket; two pillows, also of pink shag, looking like furry angels' wings, were propped against the headboard, just over her bare and smoothly rounded shoulders. A mirror showed the back of her as she leaned into the white Yeti microphone she was holding; a fluffy grey windscreen covered its grill. Pink bear-eared headphones along with a flower barrette held back all but two tendrils of the light crimson waves of her hair.

She wore a white and red lace-trimmed tank top dotted with ripe ratfruit, and below, seen more clearly in the mirror's image behind her, were matching panties.

Dolly's red lips slowly kissed the mic. She nibbled at it, closed her eyes and ran her mouth from side to side over the furred covering; she exhaled into it, sighing. She smirked. Liam saw the triangle of strawberry marks on her chest. Dolly ran her fingers through the windscreen, looked at herself on a monitor off-camera, and then stared into the camera's depths, into the future, through both time and space, as if from a universe away, at and into Liam. Her fingernails were red, too.

She bent forward, breathed heavily, and Liam breathed along with her. She sat back and pushed aside the tendrils of her hair. Her body gently swayed back and forth.

"Do you like it like that?" she whispered, and bit her bottom lip.

Dolly rubbed the laced fabric of her tank top, and then her breasts; they were long and sensual caresses. She fingered the top's straps, then pulled them over her shoulders to let them fall. She pulled the mic near to her, against her chest, stroked it, then lowered the tip below her exposed breasts. In the room's dim light, the colour of her nipples matched that of her hair, and she pressed them against the mic. Liam could hear them become erect. She flicked them lightly, tugged at and twisted them, grabbed them fully with her hands. There were dimples at the corners of her mouth, and the mic crackled as a loud and lingering moan escaped.

She opened and closed her mouth. Her tongue made alveolar clicks. She inhaled, gasped in a series of short bursts, and giggled. She licked at the air.

Dolly reached between her legs, over her panties, pressed, and closed her eyes. She brought out a veiny seven-inch dildo; her hand gripped its base and she held it near her face; she looked at the camera, then at herself, and then back. She briefly sucked on its tip, brushed her hair away again, lapped at it with her tongue, then resumed sucking. Her mouth was audibly wet, and Liam's headphones slurped and squelched, like walking in water-filled rubber boots. She spat on its head. She pushed it further into her mouth, to the back of her throat; she grunted musically, and went faster. She tapped the dildo against the mic, looked at the camera and laughed, then returned it to her mouth.

Dolly put down the mic, pressed her breasts together with her upper arms, and began to jerk off the dildo. She bounced slightly as she did, and her breasts bounced along with her.

And it was at that point that Liam, seeing the full extent of Dolly's torso – her neck and shoulders, the outlines of her clavicles, her naked breasts and the upper part of her stomach – that he noticed the other strawberry marks on her body. There was the triangle that pointed to her cleavage, yes, but on the underside of her left breast, and slightly below her nipple, was another; and the more Liam looked, the more he stared, the more he could see; and it was as if he were looking up at the night's sky, as if his eyes needed time to adjust to see the wonders that it held: its stars, its constellations. There was another near her right armpit, and others, lighter-coloured ones, faint in the room's light, that dotted the upper boundaries of her breasts. And they reminded Liam of the constellation of the great sapper.

He paused the video, found the survival handbook, and turned to the section on constellations.

*The stars have been studied for thousands of years and the groups, or constellations, in which they appear to the naked eye were named in ancient times after animals and plants and mythological figures that their shape suggested. Some, like the great sapper constellation, are useful navigational aids and were used by ancient nadanians as a guide to know the angle or degree at which to jump from asteroid to asteroid, many of which still correspond to the major settlements of today. For example, the lower right star (circled in the illustration below) will lead one to Rock Nippan. Although modern advances have supplanted the need for such navigational aids, they are useful to know if all else fails.*

Liam held up the book's illustration to the paused video and compared the two. There were slight differences, but they were remarkably similar; so much so that Liam marveled that the mark just below Dolly's right nipple corresponded to the star that led to Rock Nippan.

Liam unpaused the video, and the universe, and all it contained, was once again set in motion.

Dolly pulled on the dildo. She rubbed and slapped it against the starry heavens of her breasts and body. A thin sheen of saliva glistened on it, and, gripped in her hands, it sounded like soap being lathered.

She bent forward, toward the mic, and again took it in her mouth. She pushed it in and out aggressively, as if she were brushing her teeth, or the base of her tongue, with it. She let it out with a pop, inhaled sharply, pinched her nipple, and then sucked it again, twisting it in her mouth, moaning. When she popped it out again, a pulse of spit came with it, and it dripped onto her chin. Dolly slurped it back. She attacked the dildo playfully with her teeth. She licked its shaft and flitted its head. Its rubber balls slapped against her cheek and chin. She kissed it loudly. Forcibly. Gratuitously. She panted into the mic. And then slowly, as if to extend the pleasure of it, Dolly slid the dildo into her mouth one last time. And then slowly out. She smiled knowingly.

"Thank you for watching this," she said, her voice held a soft lilt. "I hope you enjoyed it a lot."

Dolly fluffed the windscreen with her fingers. Breathed into it and in and out. And kissed Liam goodbye.

*Mason Decision, 329PC*. Rick Mason was charged for cone licing out of season with an illegal net and then selling the lice without a permit. His conviction was reversed when the court recognized the handshake treaties, and thereafter provided nadanian cone licers access to commercial liceries.

# 6

The air was cool and thin on Seven Breezes when Liam next went to check on the bottle trap. The cloudlake, from what he could tell, had been thick the previous evening, and the handbook said that was a promising sign. But when he pulled on the line to bring it down, Liam's optimism dissolved. Not only was there no blackfish inside, but the bait was gone as well.

He released the bottle, still on its line, back into the cloudlake and went inside, where he flipped through the handbook to find something else to make. His choices were limited and Liam looked at the chef's knife. It was sharp, but wouldn't provide the control and versatility that the buck knife had, and so Liam searched for something that the twenty-centimeter S-series Zwilling Professional could handle. He decided to make rope.

*Hiss nettles are an excellent source of fibre but require preparation. Choose the oldest available nettles and those with the longest stems. Soak them in water for twenty-four hours, and then lay them on the ground and pound them with a smooth stone. This will shred the outer surface and expose the fibrous center. Tease and comb to remove the fleshly matter, and hang to dry. Once dry, remove and discard the outer layer and spin the fibres into long threads, plaiting or twisting them together to make the rope.*

Liam put on a sweater under the Snuggie, found a pair of pastel green gardening gloves, a totebag, and, holding the Zwilling as if it were a machete, hiked up the trail that led up the asteroid's north end. He passed through the knot quills bearded with epiphytic punchplants, around the outcrops covered with splatfern, to the thicket of hiss nettles. He stood silent, motionless, and listened. It was early in the season. The hissing would get increasingly louder as summer approached, but Liam could hear the faint beginnings of it; like stale air was escaping through hundreds of tiny holes in an ever-shriveling, never-depleted balloon.

Liam studied his surroundings. The space was relatively open, sprinkled with a few jelly quills, lone and dying. Walking through it was hazardous due to the pickle vines, which would ensnare the foot and cause one to tumble. There were also several downed quills obscured beneath – the combination could easily result in a twisted or broken ankle. Within the green sea of hiss nettles, there were ratfruit and cutweed in small tufts, singly stalked flowers that would soon turn into bullet berries; there were sun tails and horn bladders and a thin layer of sheet moss. Given the nettles' abundance, Liam had no qualms harvesting them. He figured about fifty stalks would give him a good amount of rope.

Using the Zwilling to cut away at the tangle of pickle vines, Liam cleared a passage to the largest hiss nettles. They were several metres tall. He severed them at their bases, ran his gloved hands over their stems from top to bottom, and, realizing the tote bag was useless for holding stems so long, instead tied its handles around the stalks to make a bundle. Not wanting to traipse back through the tangle, Liam slashed his way to the nearest highest ground.

He circled around and back to the trail that would return him to the cottage.

Up ahead, he saw the snapped bole of the giant sapseed. Using it as a bearing, he stumbled into the clearing at the sapseed's base.

And there he froze, startled by what he saw. The dark mouth of the den was there, but at its dirty lip, with not a trace of disturbance, no tracks, no impressions of either foot or claw, there rested a bag. Purple, cloth, gold-coloured drawstring pulled tight to enclose its contents. He looked around cautiously. The cameras were there, but they'd been moved, angled away from their previous positions. One pointed directly at the den's entrance. *Mouth, not entrance,* Liam thought. *It was a mouth.*

He dropped the bundle, gripped the Zwilling tight, and unsheathed his phone to download the images. Nothing. He went to one, opened the front, and saw that the storage card was missing. He went to the other and saw the same. He turned on the phone's flashlight, slowly walked up to the den, and kicked the purple bag back toward the bundle of nettles. The mass inside clinked and jingled where it landed. Liam pointed the phone down the hole, illuminating its throat. It went down several feet before turning, but there, at the bottom, at the bend, were his cameras' storage cards. The beam of the phone's light reflected off their gold pins.

The Baited Hole Noose.

*Digging pits disturbs the environment and leaves a permanent mark. This will alarm some animals. In others, curiosity may outweigh discretion and they will investigate. Baiting the hole may bring animals sniffing.*

Liam backed away, toward the bundle and bag, and picked up both. Coins, he thought. He loosened the golden drawstring and looked inside. There were coins, pennies, small plastic discs used in games of rummoli, and settled inside with it all was a candle and a folding knife – *his* folding knife. A DeWalt with a ten-centimeter stainless steel partially-serrated blade and wire stripper.

Liam pocketed the knife, glanced again at the hole, then followed the trail out. It's said that there are some who know when they're being watched, that they can feel the weight of perception on them, eyeing them up and down, assessing, gauging, analyzing their behaviour, their reactions. Liam felt nothing of the sort. He felt alone. Isolated. Invisible. And that's what made it all the more unnerving. Because he knew it wasn't so.

At the cottage, he threw the nettle stalks into the bathtub and ran water to fill it. He took the bag and placed it on the kitchen table, less wary given he knew what it contained, but only a little less so. He removed the candle and set it down beside the bag of coins. He knew what it was and knew its purpose.

It was a nadanian ceremonial candle. Its wax was from the crystalized sap of the giant sapseed, and it took forever to make; first to find the giant sapseed, then to harvest the sap, which must be done when its fruits have not yet matured. The crystallization process is lengthy, too, and takes patience and care; and then there is its candling. It was used in purification rituals, to prepare an ahkeh for their spiritual journey, to help them make a wise decision, or to invoke the dream world. The only thing a candle should invoke is light and heat, thought Liam.

Liam picked it up and smelled it. Slightly sweet. The smell of a meadow in autumn. A trace of smoke. A honeyed lip balm. But mostly like nothing. Like paraffin wax.

He found a barbeque lighter in a basket atop the pantry, then went into the bathroom and set the candle on the edge of the tub. He stirred and soaked the nettles in warm water and lit the candle. He sat on the toilet's lid and watched it burn. Sapseed wax dripped from its stiff wick, which appeared to be from a part of the giant sapseed, too – its trunk hairs perhaps, or maybe from thin strands of hiss nettles. It burned clean, the sweet smell markedly amplified when lit. Liam closed the door and flipped the switch, surprised by the amount of light the candle cast.

The flame flickered like a devil dancing on the head of a pin, as if there was a shifting of air, a gust of wind, as if a door had been opened. It shuddered, flailed on the drowning wick.

There was a noise, the door to the outside opening and closing, and Liam turned toward the sound. He strained to hear anything more over the accompanying silence.

"Liam," whispered someone from the bathtub, and he turned back.

There lay Dolly Lilith, submerged alongside the nettles, their long, thin stalks draped over her breasts and stomach. She stared at Liam, leaned toward the candle and its flame, pursed her lips as if to kiss it, and blew.

"You're doing so well, my lovely," she said in the darkness.

And Liam was pulled into the tub and under the water, where he swirled down into the drain, into the den, the mouth, the throat, the ravenous, waiting stomach of Ahmem.

\*\*\*

He landed with a wet thud. The ground sagged like a sponge under his weight. Dark. Too dark to see. Water. Or saliva. Pools around his hands and knees. Liam crawled through it. A tongue. Towards. *My lovely.* Towards what. Pluck. *Towards me.* And you are. *Closer, my lovely.* Through screaming hiss nettles. Through a bed of nipples. The smell of boiled pennies. Whiskey and wine. A shot glass full of vomit. Panties. *I'm so happy that you're here.* The sound of crinkling tin foil. *Closer.* Pluck. *It's really good to see you.* And I am. *You're doing really well.*

Liam saw a light and crawled toward it. His phone. Vibrating. Jenn's voice. Liam. Jenn. *Liam, they're coming. They're in the next room.* Who is? Jenn? Jenn, answer me. *Shhhhhh. Liam, they're going to find me. I couldn't save them, Liam. I couldn't save them.* Save who, Jenn? Save who? Jenn? Jenn? Please answer me, Jenn. The call dropped. Pluck.

*You can do such wonderful things.* Where am I? *You're so special.* Where's Jenn? Somewhere a snare tightened. A trap tripped. An animal struggled. And died. I am not animal. *Nor am I.* What are you? *Closer.* The phone's light flickered like a candle. No walls. Pluck. No ceiling. Just the stars. An unimaginable distance.

From Jenn. So slow. Eternity enclosed in the spin of marble. *Shhhhhh.* Jenn? *Shhhhhh, Liam. You're doing so well.* Jenn where are you? *Closer.*

At a distance, a bathtub. *Here I am, my lovely.* Jenn? *My lovely.* A claw scraped against metal. Splashed. Liam moved closer. Pluck. A leg emerged. Segmented. Over the tub's edge. Spines. Like lithe needles. Hairs. A har. *My lovely.* You're the first one. Another leg. Another claw. *I'm the only one.* A spiner. *Shhhhhh. I'm so proud of you.* Another leg. Claw. Six. It stepped out. Relax. Water fell from its body, into the tub. Drip. Pluck. *Let me in, Liam.* The spiner unfolded. Expanded. The tub was a marble. *Liam. Closer.* What do you want? *To let you in.* Pluck.

It turned and on its body, as if her skin clung to it like clothes, was Dolly Lilith. Her face was stretched grotesquely, her body worn like a hide, spread out across the spiner, her breasts pulled flat against its scaled exoskeleton. Her strawberry marks expanded into saucer-sized red-brown puddles. Her lips were like pinned slugs, a mass of gelatin tossed onto the floor, and they moved. *My lovely.* They whispered. *You're doing such a good job.*

Dolly moved toward Liam. Her arms, like maxillary palps, drew him near. Her hands caressed his face. *Shhhhhh.* Fingers ran through his hair. Pluck. Across his cheek. Into his mouth. *You're safe now.* She took his hand in hers and sucked on a finger. Spit dripped from her distended lips. He could feel the warmth of her insides. Could hear her slurp. Her tongue tasted him. She opened her mouth wide. His hand rubbed against her uvula. His forearm. Elbow. Liam breathed. Relaxed.

There was no pain when she bit down. Only an intense desire to be loved. To be consumed. To give his life toward something larger. Than himself. Than the world. Than *any* world.

He cried with joy when his arm was swallowed whole. And Dolly licked up every tear. Pluck.

When Liam woke, the inside of his red Snuggie was filled with ejaculate.

*Gar Nation Decision, 334PC.* Gar-Nada transferred a quill farm licence from one company to another. Gar Nation argued that they held title and claim to the licenced area. The case clarified that there was an obligation for the Universal Government to consult with nadanian nations prior to any decision that could infringe on their rights.

# 7

Liam was at the den. He pushed himself up off the ground. His pants were damp, his shoes missing, pieces of quill feathers and dried mud clung to his sides and thighs. His skin felt like it had been thrashed by hiss nettles, a series of small red welts ran up and along his arms. He pulled up the front of the Snuggie to inspect his chest and saw welts there, too. They looked like teeth marks.

He patted his pockets and felt the buck knife inside. And then, in a panic, realized he was without an oxygen mask. His breathing became laboured, as if his body had only then caught up. He took deep pulls of the asteroid's thin air and looked around with muted, increasing desperation. Slow, he said to himself, breathe in slowly, breathe in completely, and then release.

The cameras, useless without their storage cards, were where he'd left them. The hole was there, too, and Liam saw it had been disturbed, as if a wounded animal had crawled out. Him, Liam thought, the animal was him. He saw a handprint, saw where the texture of his soaked sock had left its patterned mark in the soil, where his knees scraped shallow troughs in short, scurrying bursts – all of which led to where he'd been sleeping. Where he'd collapsed.

He stepped toward the hole and cautiously peered over its lip, fearing what he might see. It was lit from within, and Liam saw his phone, its flashlight on, shining, pointing, it seemed, to his oxygen mask. He hesitated; there would be an extra mask at the cottage, but that was far from the den, too far to go without one. He coughed as he knelt and stuck his arm into the hole, into the mouth of

Ahmem. He coughed again and struggled to extend his reach as far as possible; his fingers grazed its straps.

He pulled out the mask and put it on with a quickness that surprised him, clicked the valve, heard the short *whoosh* of the canister inside releasing its contents. Liam breathed in the fullness of its clean air, gasping. Its oxygenated richness made him dizzy. Wooziness coupled with comforting relief. It was in that state that he heard a soft bang, a low *whump*, like a barbeque being lit.

For a moment, as he regained his composure, as the oxygen returned to balance and calm his thoughts, as his mind replayed what must have surely been a dream: the spiner Ahmem wearing the hide of Dolly Lilith – for a moment, he simply meditated on the sound, considered its edges, its contours, its shape and texture, its potential source, and what it could possibly mean.

When it happened again, he looked up and toward the shifting cloudlake and saw that Merlan Mykhailuk's cottage was on fire. Even at such a distance, Liam could see a large breach in its side, and flames, fed by a ruptured pipe, leaking a relentless stream of oxygen, blazed like a river of molten fangs.

He abandoned his phone and rushed down the trail to the cottage. But as he neared it, he saw that he was not alone. Merlan's ship stood upright beside his, clearly only recently landed, but in front of it was not Merlan, but a nadanian dressed in green military fatigues. There were more of them, too. One held Wilf's rifle from the upstairs closet; he stood on the short series of steps that rose to the cottage's open door. Others, three more, Liam guessed, were inside.

Liam crouched behind the copse of quills near the bedroom window and eased himself under its feathers; they cloaked him enough that he could move within earshot. The one with the rifle had a long scar, from his ear, across his jaw, to his chin. Liam recognized him as the nadanian at the Rock Enor transfer station. The land protector. The member of ARM. The one with his hundred dollars.

"There's no one here," said one of them.

"Just as well," said the land protector. "Take whatever you can find."

"They could come back."

"Who could?"

"Whoever lives here."

"No one who lives here."

"Someone was here. Look at that there."

"They don't live here now."

"Could come back. Their ship's here. Could be out in the quills."

"Go check then."

"What?"

"Go check then. You want to make sure no one's here, you go on and check then."

"The whole asteroid?"

"Whatever you want. The whole asteroid, sure. And you know what we're going to do while you're gone? The rest of us here are going to load the fat guy's ship, that means oxygen, that means water, power, everything you need to live once you're done fucking around in the quills, and we're going to leave you the fuck behind. So you want to check the entire asteroid? Be my guest, go on out and check."

"I'm just saying."

"What? What are you saying?"

"Alright then, okay, fine. He knows the fat guy, though."

"Knew."

"What?"

"Knew the fat guy."

"Knew the fat guy, yeah."

"And?"

"And nothing. I'm just saying."

"Go pull the batteries."

"From the house or the ship?"

"Both."

"What about this? It was just sitting on the bathtub."

There was a pause as the land protector looked at it.

"Leave it."

"It's valuable, you know? Rare. My ahkeh said that it's –"

"I said leave it. Pull the power. Load the ship. We're leaving. And put that back where you found it. And, Connor, I want you to listen to me very carefully, put it back exactly where you found it."

"On the tub?"

"Is that where you found it?"

"Well, yeah. It was just sitting there, and I know what it is, my ahkeh says that –"

"You don't know what it is."

"What?"

"I said you don't know what it is."

"It's a sapseed candle. One of the medicines."

"No."

"Well then what is it?"

"Something that means whoever was here is already dead."

"Alright, but what is it?"

"Just pull the batteries."

Liam listened and could hardly believe what he heard. Had ARM really killed Merlan? They had destroyed his home. And by taking everything, they'd be leaving Liam for dead, too.

The land protector loaded Wilf's rifle. Liam knew that the attached black-plastic magazine could hold roughly ten bullets, and the land protector pulled back the bolt to chamber one of them. He aimed at the windshield of Liam's ship and fired. A web of cracks spread from where it hit the glass. He pulled the bolt back again and fired, the shot penetrated the glass and disappeared into the passenger's seat. The small opening it left behind was, in Liam's mind, as large as a black hole.

Liam could do nothing but watch. The ARM members pulled the batteries from his ship and the cottage; they took oxygen tanks, the reserves, too; they took his water, his food, his booze: the whiskey and boxes of nadanian red wine. They loaded it all into Merlan's ship. One emerged from under Liam's ship with a knife, having cut something, covered in a bluish liquid. They powered up Merlan's ship. The land protector, standing beside it, looked up the trail to the rising hill of the asteroid's north end, to the gradual slope down to the edge of the cloudlake, then back to the cottage. His gaze stopped at the copse of quills under which Liam hid. He stared. Then he aimed and fired one last shot at the small sign that hung just above the cottage's doorway, the one that read *Welcome to Seven Breezes*. Then they left. The moss around the landing pad was a charred shadow.

Liam stayed where he was, crouched under the quills' lush feathers. He looked out at the cloud, and beyond to Merlan's asteroid, which had become engulfed in a grey haze. The fire spread from the cottage to the adjacent quills.

When Liam entered the Seven Breezes cottage, passing under its damaged sign, the *O* in *Welcome* now shot out, he expected to see a mess – the contents of drawers and cabinets turned out and onto the floor, furniture upended or cut open, the TV smashed for no reason – but the place was, for the most part, just as he'd left it.

He walked around in a haunted silence. The water and batteries were gone. There was no hum of the baseboard heaters. No drone from the water recycling system. It would soon be cold and dark. They'd taken his booze. An empty gun case lay open on the bed upstairs, a few stray bullets scattered inside, some on the bed's covers, some on the floor. Liam scooped them up and tossed them into the case with the others.

He went back down to the main floor, into the bathroom. The sapper candle was there, planted on the tub's edge. Hung over the shower curtain rod was a double-plaited rope made of hiss nettles. The bathtub water, about the same amount Liam had put in earlier, was cloudy. Liam dipped his fingers into it. Still warm. He pulled down the rope and examined it. About four metres long. He took the rope and the candle into the living room and put them on the coffee table. He sat on the couch and found the survival handbook wedged between two cushions, and put that on the table too.

How long had he been dreaming? *Had* he been dreaming? Liam looked at his hands as if he'd find some sign in them that proved he'd made the rope. There was dirt under his fingernails, but no cuts, no abrasions, no blisters. If he didn't make the rope, then who did? Certainly not ARM, not the land protector. And what was wrong with the sapper candle? Why did the land protector think he was already dead?

It was all too much.

A flash at the corner of his eye caught Liam's attention. He turned and looked out across the vastness of the cloudlake. A pulse of light flashed from the Seidelskyys' asteroid. Liam went to the telescope and looked through the eyepiece. He saw green military fatigues. He saw the land protector with Wilf's gun. He saw Merlan's ship. What he didn't see was Dolly Lilith. The lights of the Sedielskyy's cottage were on and he could see dark figures moving around inside, ARM members, but no one who looked like Dolly. About ten minutes later, the lights went out. The ship started up, launched into the cloudlake, and disappeared behind it.

Liam looked for movement and, seeing none, was overcome with a sense of helplessness. A hopelessness the size of Gar-Nada. He was alone. And there was nothing he could do. His phone was at the bottom of a pit. He was without power, without any way of contacting others. What happened to Merlan? Dolly? What will happen to him?

A pitiful panic began to well within him. In an effort to keep it from pouring out, to keep some form of control, however small, he ran to the powerroom to look for something, anything, that could help. Gone. It was all gone. He ran to the bedroom and pillaged the drawers and closet. Nothing. He went under the stairs, thinking there must be something the nadanians had missed, but all he found were buckets, a vacuum cleaner, and old linens. He ran upstairs, picked up the gun case, and threw it hard against the wall. What have you done, Liam? What kind of mess have you got yourself into? He breathed. Deeply and deliberately. Slowly, a semblance of composure returned.

The radio, he thought, and he rummaged through the closet's shelves, pushing away board games and puzzle boxes, until he found it: the FosPower solar crank portable radio.

He went back downstairs, quickly checked the telescope, then began to crank the handle that charged the radio. It wouldn't allow for a distress call, but at least it was something. If he could figure out what was happening, well, then, that could help, couldn't it? Something must be going on. And the radio wasn't nothing, right? It'd help, he thought, sincerely. Desperately. It'd help.

Liam stopped, turned up the volume, twisted the tuning dial until it crackled. He turned it back slowly, as if the signal needed to be trapped, and found the Universal Government's station. He sat on the couch and listened to the broadcaster's voice.

"...in an unprecedented vote at today's parliamentary session, Rock Nippan MP, Chloe Troughburn, tabled her motion calling on the Universal Government to recognize Nada's phrontistery dwellings as genocide. The motion passed unanimously.

"'In light of the detection of possible unobserved burials of little nadanians at Rock Paradox, this vote today is historic,' said Troughburn. 'I want to thank them, the little ones, and I want to let them know that they are not forgotten. I want them to know they are important and that their lives mattered and that we – Nada and the Universal Government – now recognize their sacrifice for what it truly was: genocide.'

"To honour the motion's adoption, the Universal Government said they will fly Nada's flag at half mast and..."

Liam wept into his hands as the fire consumed the Seidelskyys' cottage.

*Pym Nation Decision, 344PC.* Several nomadic nadanians objected to quill harvesting on what they claimed were their ancestral asteroids. Courts found that Pym Nation had a beneficial interest in the asteroids even though the Universal Government retained their control. As a result, nadanian title did not require regular occupation for it to exist.

# 8

That night, Liam didn't sleep. He tossed about on the couch and the oxygen mask pushed up awkwardly on his face as he turned this way and that; he feared he'd break the seal, that he'd waste it, and he needed as much oxygen as he could get. He feared what he would have to do to survive, if he even could survive until help came, if help came. What if it didn't? What then? He feared the nadanian land protectors would return, what they would do upon returning, who else they would bring, what they would bring with them. But still he tried to sleep. To no avail.

Eventually, as the diffused light of dawn approached, Liam gave up trying and merely sat there on the couch looking at the contents strewn upon the coffee table: the knife, the candle, the rope, the radio, the handbook. He picked up the book and read.

*Water, food, fire, and shelter – these are your basic needs, and, if you are prepared, only in rare cases would they be lacking in the environment.*

So this is what it has come to, thought Liam. This is the promise of the civilized world: to have all one's basic needs met. Liam stared at the words until they lost all their meaning.

He went to the fridge and looked inside. There were condiments, a half jar of olives, dried dates, two green onions, and a loaf of bread. He pulled open the freezer, saw it was empty, and shut it again. He went to the pantry with mounting unease, exhaled, a tenseness sloughing from his shoulders when he saw it was mostly untouched. One shelf was still full of stacked cans – tomato paste, tuna, brown lentils, a can of sliced mushrooms. Another shelf held a small tin of sugar, a larger one held flour. Perhaps the nadanians had meant to take it, thought Liam as he closed the pantry door. Perhaps they still did.

Liam went to the bathroom and looked at the tub. The water remained, still cloudy but slightly less so, much of its suspended sediment having settled to the bottom. He got a glass from the kitchen and scooped up a small portion of water. He held it up to the light of the window and saw it was tinged yellow. Little flecks of something swirled inside. He hoped the colour was due to the soaking hiss nettles and not because one of the nadanians pissed in it. It smelled like water. Tub water, but water nonetheless. He took a sip and tasted nothing foul. What choice did he have? He drank the rest, and, realizing his thirst was great, dipped the glass to its brim and drank again. He'd need to conserve it, though. For all he knew, this could be the only water on Seven Breezes.

It took Liam a moment to find the barbeque lighter, as it had fallen behind the toilet. But there it was, and it still worked. Barely.

Fire, water, food. And the cottage would provide for a more than adequate shelter. He pulled off his oxygen mask and checked the pressure gauge. Two days worth, maybe three. Liam forcibly steadied his breathing. There was no need to panic. Not yet. What had the book said about basic needs? *Only in rare cases would they be lacking in the environment.* Liam wasn't a rare case. Not yet. He'd find more, somewhere, even if it was risky. And what else did the book say? *The final risk is yours to make, and no one will blame you if it is the wrong one.* But I will, thought Liam, I'll blame me. *Not if you're dead, you won't.*

Liam ate a few pieces of bread by the window and looked out at the cloudlake. Both Merlan's and Dolly's asteroids were still covered in a smoky haze, as if they were big and fuzzy grey cocoons. He sat at the kitchen table and opened the handbook.

*The oxygen vent takes advantage of an asteroid's continuous production of dark oxygen. This method is more effective in the summer when an asteroid's oxy-*

gen production peaks. In their core, the majority of Nada's asteroids contain a labyrinth of metallic nodules, which act as large batteries, called geobatteries. As winter's ice melts, hydrolysis occurs, and the process creates a reliable source of oxygen. Oxygen vents are typically long fissures in rocks, which allow for their transportation to the surface. Once an oxygen vent is identified, build a well-sealed shelter around it to capture and concentrate the dark oxygen. This method is dependent on an asteroid's dark oxygen production and should not be relied upon for long-term use.

Liam opened a can of tuna and, with bread, pressed its contents into the shape of a sandwich. He grabbed the knife from the table, looped the rope around his neck and under his arm, and walked up the hill to the asteroid's north end to look for oxygen vents. On the way, he passed by the den and looked down its hole. His phone was gone. It had been leaning against the side of the tunnel, near where it bent into the darkness, but it was gone. Something had moved it.

Liam continued past the den, deeper into the quills. He knew there were rock outcrops in that direction, and it seemed like his best chance to locate a vent. He pushed his way through knot quills, startling a rain eel that hid in its feathers, which then swam away into the frenetic sky. Pipe fingers poked holes in a slate of sheet moss. As Liam reached the outcrop – a clearing pocked with the occasional inkwort – he found himself in a murmuration of immature cone lice. They were so thick he had to swat them away from his face to see. When they dispersed, he studied the abundance of potential vents; there were cracks everywhere. He went to one and followed the book's instructions: he pulled off his oxygen mask and held his nose to the ground. He was to inhale slowly and pay close attention to the smell and feel of it in his nostrils. Liam searched for a faintly chloridic smell, like that of a swimming pool. He neither smelled nor felt anything of the sort, and so he pulled on his mask and looked for the next crack to inspect. He went from one to the next for some time. He sat on a small boulder at the center of the clearing. He ate the sandwich and drank from a bottle of yellow tub water. He'd found nothing yet, nothing worth making a trap over. He put what he didn't eat back into the bag and continued his search, pressing his face to the rocks, hoping to inhale the smell of summer. But it seemed a waste of time. By the time the day began to wane, the only thing Liam smelled was the stagnancy of death. His own, he was sure. And so, he passed back through the knot quills to the den.

It was as he had left it. Only now, with evening approaching, it was much darker, so the hole was as bottomless as Liam's mind allowed. He took out what remained of his sandwich and placed it near the den. Liam wasn't quite sure why. What would have happened to him if he was in the cottage when the land protectors arrived? Would they have burned it down like they did Merlan's place? Like they did to the Seidelskyys'? Would they kill him like they did Merlan? Like Dolly? Did he think it was the den that saved him? Did he think he owed it something in return? For each question he asked, Liam had no answer. He didn't even know if Dolly was dead. *But of course she's dead*, was his own inevitable reply. He left the piece of sandwich where it lay.

Back at the cottage, he ate olives out of the jar, spooning them out two at a time, chewing them like salty eyeballs. The last light of the nearest stars faded and the night bloomed all around him. He exerted himself too much. His oxygen level was down more than he'd expected. He'd need to regulate his breathing.

Liam began to meditate. He focused on his breath. Felt the mask's air enter his nose, down his throat and into his lungs. He felt his chest rise, his stomach expand. He was present where he sat. The couch was beneath him; he focused on the pressure he felt, the way it held him. He felt his feet and toes, the floor and carpet beneath them. He breathed out and his focus extended to as many parts of that experience as it could. Just take slow and deliberate breaths. One at a time.

The sound that jolted him out of his meditation was as if a baseball had smashed through the window. When he opened his eyes, he saw nothing but night's insidious darkness wrapped around him. He fumbled for the barbeque lighter and blindly swept his hands across the coffee table for the candle. Liam's heart pounded, and it dismayed him that he could do nothing to control it.

He lit the candle and held it in front of him as he looked for the source of the sound. Had the land protectors returned?

Liam walked to the door and held the candle to the window. Two adirondack chairs were on the small porch, one of them was knocked over. He opened the door and looked closer. The chair was covered in black mucus, and little gnarled seeds were embedded in the sickly thick jelly. It was a splatfern. Not ARM. Not the land protector back to finish the job. Just a splatfern. It was nothing. It happened all the time.

Liam returned to the couch and stared at the candle in his hand. He was burning up what little oxygen he had. The small flame flickered, as if it, too, agreed and wished to be snuffed. Liam watched it a moment longer and then blew it out.

In the darkness, a thin trail of smoke slithered into the air and disappeared. And Liam's consciousness disappeared with it.

\*\*\*

In his dream, he was back at the outcrop clearing and stood before a small fire pit. Fist-sized stones were arranged in a circle, surrounding a bed of ash. Liam held out his hand and felt its warmth. He looked out to the periphery of the clearing, to the knot quills and beyond, where the rock's outcrop dove under a blanket of moss and soil. "Hello," he called, "who's there?" The air was full of nothingness, like everything in it had been siphoned away; only a void remained. His voice echoed silently.

Liam stomped out the dying embers. He unzipped his pants and urinated on it. The pit hissed and sent up large plumes of opaque smoke. It engulfed him, clung to his face, he coughed as he tasted its sourness; it was the taste of boiled blood, burning extension cords, as if molten glass had been splashed onto his skin.

Liam heard them before he saw them. The saparians. They chittered, a thick clicking sound, emerging from deep with their throats rather than their tongues. A dozen of them, maybe more, surrounded him. They were small, hooded creatures with shrouds of quill feathers, mud and moss, pounded, woven together, patternless. Their faces were impossible to see in the dim light, but Liam knew they were slug-like, covered in black pubescence. Their breathing traveled from foot to head, reminding Liam of segmented tube fleas, of how a wave of moving legs would sweep from one end to the other as it crawled into the cracked seams of the asteroid's granitic bones. They swelled from the ground up. Vaguely, yet not at all, humanian.

Liam's body abandoned him. His muscles froze. His eyes and lids remained motionless, compelled to stay open. Even when he fell to the ground, as the knot quills slashed sideways across his vision, his eyes never closed. Long fingers pressed against them from behind, and Liam felt as if he'd become a glove, like someone were thumbing through his brain, reading him. Liam was a dull and empty husk. His mind was stirred into a slurry, ready to be sucked out with a straw.

The fire pit fell into itself to reveal the long and winding tunnel of the den, and then a clawed and handless limb pulled him in.

***

The sound of a smoke alarm caused Liam to open his eyes, and he saw he was still sitting on the couch in front of the long-extinguished candle. It was his mask that was screaming. Running out of oxygen. A button on the side muted its piercing cries. He should have panicked, and it relieved him to know that he wasn't. The saparians had come to Liam in a dream, and they had shown him what he had to do.

He grabbed a box of black garbage bags from under the kitchen sink. He removed the grill from the barbeque. He found duct tape and tent pegs and, with his oxygen mask chirping every thirty seconds, hauled it all up the trail to the den.

He started to build an oxygen trap. He put the grill over the hole, secured it to the ground with tent pegs, and duct-taped several black bags together. He used rocks to hold the base of the garbage bags in place and wrapped and taped and pinched it all together into a rough cone shape, the top of which he taped to the side of the giant sapseed looming over it all. Liam entered the oxygen trap and taped the flap shut behind him. He inspected the seams and, satisfied, cut out a venthole near the trap's narrow top with his knife. It was large enough to lay in, but no larger. Liam stooped, mindful of the grill and the hole it covered. Kneeling in the trap, he removed his mask. The black walls faintly mimicked his breath; they pulled inward as he inhaled, extended out as he exhaled. He bent forward and put his face, his nose, to the grill. In the clearing, each fissure was fragrant with the scent of stone, but the den was different. He smelled a swimming pool in summer. He smelled chlorine. Dark Oxygen. But would it be enough, he wondered. It would have to be.

Liam closed his eyes and concentrated. He thought of the sound of fabric rustling, of fingernails zig-zagging down the zipper of his spine, of Dolly's combed hair. *You're doing so well, my lovely.* Liam regulated his breath. In and out.

***

Only when he woke the next morning did he realize he'd been sleeping. His mask lay across from him. Starlight shone through the venthole above, and it passed through the slats of the grill into the darkness below. The ghost of a wind flapped against the garbage bag walls. There was light behind their darkness.

Liam breathed deeply. He had a slight headache, but was alive. He had survived the night without an oxygen mask and, for the first time in several days, he felt rested. Surprisingly, it had worked.

Liam knew he had to ration the mask's oxygen. As far as he knew, only in the trap could he take it off. With it on, he went back to the cottage and gathered as much food as he could. He filled several bottles with tub water and hauled it all back to the trap. The mask continued to beep, warning him to be careful.

He reinforced the trap's walls with additional bags, ringed the base with additional rocks, then simply sat inside.

*Survival is the art of staying alive. You must be able to maintain your morale. Your confidence will enable you to overcome fear, boredom, isolation, and loneliness.*

What he couldn't eat, Liam dropped through the grill into infinite darkness. He returned to the cottage for more supplies. He meditated in the trap. He focused on his breath.

And then one day, a day that arrived all too soon, the food was gone. The cans were empty, the cupboards bare, the bathtub dry.

He checked the bottle traps and found some had caught blackfish minnows; they shimmered like opalescent shadows. Liam ate them raw, crunching them dead between his teeth. He spit some of the paste into empty bottles as bait and released them back into the cloud. And then his mask fell silent. Empty. He could travel a minute's radius from the den, any more and he risked hypoxia. Even so, he'd return to the trap gasping and light-headed.

He uncoiled a small portion of rope to use as a snare. He set up several along scat bear trails. He carved a trigger bar and upright out of a knot quill sapling, stripped another of its feathers, and bent it down to lock them all together. The spring snare he placed along the path of a quill slug. They were difficult to set up, and several times he had to abandon them to recover in the oxygen trap. Even when he succeeded, when he set the snare perfectly, ready to trap a passing slug or bear, he'd return to find them broken, crushed under some giant foot. It was as if the asteroid wished him dead.

He scoured the immediate area for edible plants. There were a few ratfruit, which he quickly devoured. Some hareberries. He chewed and sucked on a sun tail stalk. Its juices lessened his thirst, but Liam knew it was not enough to sustain him.

Hunger snuck up like a prawn fisher. His stomach growled demandingly, but stopped after some time, as if his stomach knew it was useless to continue to beg. As if it had accepted that it would never again know that simple easy pleasure.

In the darkness of his desperation, Liam placed the candle in the center of the grill. He knew what lighting it would mean and yet did it anyway.

\*\*\*

He was once again plunged into the world of dreams. His body transformed into that of a spiner. Clawed appendages replaced his legs, sleek and spiked with dangerously sharp hairs, and they held up his bulky exoskeleton like girdered beams. His ribbed thorax narrowed into a short and powerful neck, covered in spines, frilling a head that looked neither nadanian nor saparian, but far more ancient. He was a spine person, a har, one of the original ur-nadans.

He crashed through the knot and jelly quills with ease, their outstretched feathers frail against his substantial weight, snapping in his wake. It was little effort to breathe, as if oxygen were coming through every pore, like thousands of tiny mouths feeding thousands of tiny lungs.

A scat bear darted before him and he lunged and snapped at it with his beak; he felt it struggle briefly in his jaws, then swallowed it in two short gulps. The trill of a quill slug sounded overhead. Liam's long and taloned limb pierced its side. Its death squeak was short as it crunched in Liam's mouth. He pressed himself into a ball, hiding in a mess of hiss nettles and punchplants, and waited for a school of rain eels to pass by. He drank their wet innards and swallowed their balloon-like rubbery skin. He caught several prawn fishers and ate those, too.

Liam's hunger became a distant memory.

He stalked Seven Breezes with impunity. He clambered up the steps of the cottage and bit off the blooms of the splatfern that had grown near the door. He crawled onto the roof and used it like an observational tower. The cloudlake drifted over him, and Liam watched it with all six of his eyes. It was too far for him to pluck out a blackfish or a cloudcrab, but the roof allowed for a view of the top of the quill forest. And there he saw, at the top of one of the tallest feather quills, a large nest. A molerin nest. He crawled down the side of the cottage and crept toward the tall quill. Molerin build their nests as high as possible; however, they also scavenge around the base of the quill – especially their flightless young.

Liam's clawed legs silently moved through the duff, stabbing the soil as he passed over. He saw the quill's base and froze. Beside it, a fledgling molerin flapped uselessly on the ground. Liam's eyes widened. The creature cooed stupidly and Liam reared his front legs to attack.

Something below him clicked. When he looked down, it was too late. One of the spines that jutted from his leg had tripped the trigger, and a spring-loaded spear trap released and swung into his side. The sharpened tips of two featherless quill sticks stuck themselves deep into the soft parts of his thorax. Yellow blood and green goo pooled around him as he slowly lost consciousness. As he died.

***

Back inside the oxygen trap, Liam howled himself awake.

His hunger woke, too, angrier than ever. The candle was snuffed, at rest right where he'd left it. He was parched, his mouth painfully dry. He sat there for some time to collect his thoughts. What did the dream mean? He needed food. He needed water. The traps he set had caught nothing. Less than nothing. They sapped his energy, and for what? He could continue to wait passively, but that would be waiting for death. He could become like a spiner, and hunt. But how different would that turn out? He needed something more, something bigger than a snare. Liam flipped through the survival manual. In a dream, the deadfall spear trap had caught the asteroid's largest predator. Liam would make that dream a reality.

He inhaled, opened the flap of the oxygen trap, and went outside. He was surprised to find that one of the snares had tightened around the tail of a rain eel. It thrashed exhaustedly, almost performatively, as Liam approached it. He took it back to the oxygen trap and cut out two fillets, eating one raw and setting the other aside with its offal. Its moist flesh was sweet between his cracked lips.

The other snares were empty; some were tripped, some destroyed. Though desperate, Liam knew he had to be patient. He surveyed the area, returned to the trap several times to catch his breath. He'd need to do so in stages – breathing deep, filling his lungs with the trap's faint supply, going back and forth as needed, as his breaths became shallower and shallower, and as he became weaker and weaker – but he knew what he had to do.

He pulled a rotting (yet sturdy) knot quill bole under a thick, overhanging quill. He snapped saplings and carved their wider ends into pointed spears, which, along with a large rock, he fastened to the end of the quill bole with the nettle rope. He threw the loose end around the overhanging quill and pulled, raising the killing end. He let it down lightly again. He studied the short stubs of old expended feathers that dotted the base of the quill bole, and he cut the retaining bar out of one of the shed quills. He held the carved bar to the bole stubs and fed the rope through to test its trigger. He pulled it taut and the bar held; he pulled harder and the bar released. He pulled the loose end of the rope over an animal trail and tied it to the base of a quill. He lifted the downed quill and leaned it against a long quill-log, set upright, as he returned the retaining bar to its bole stubs, over top of the rope, with enough tension that it held in place. He got under the bole, used his shoulder to lift it slightly, and kicked out the temporary crutch that had held it, and, slowly bending his knees, lowered the deadfall into place, arming it. The speared end stayed, the retaining bar held, and Liam stood back and watched it. He inhaled shallowly and feared even that may set it off.

It was exhausting work and Liam sat in the oxygen trap for several hours to regain himself. He ate the remaining fillet. Perhaps it was all in his mind, but the air that rose up from the hole was richer. Come summer, he may no longer need the trap. But that was still weeks away, at least, probably more.

Liam grabbed the pile of offal and returned to the deadfall trap. It remained set. The two teeth of its upper jaw waited to snap shut. Carefully, he slid the offal under the rope, just below where the teeth would bite.

What is the meaning behind our dreams? Should we look to them for guidance? Are they visions of the future? Do they teach us anything of value? Or are we simply making connections where none exist?

"Liam," whispered Dolly.

A long-fingered hand, gaunt and thin-wristed, veins like branching strands of algae, reached out from around the standing quill and flicked the retaining bar loose.

Liam fell backwards, but the deadfall fell even quicker, and its teeth caught his calf and pinned him to the ground.

*Rat Fruit Decision, 351PC*. Rat Fruit Nation challenged the Universal Government, claiming it did not take into account the cumulative effects of multiple resource extraction projects and that there were no longer sufficient and appropriate asteroids on which to meaningfully exercise their rights. Courts found favour with the Nation and awarded $400 million in compensation.

# 9

*Pain is a warning signal that calls attention to an injury or physical condition. It is not in itself dangerous, however distressing and discomforting it can be. Pain can be controlled and overcome. Concentration and intense effort can work to stop and reduce feelings of pain for a time, though, it is important to treat any injury as soon as possible.*

Liam cut the rope that fastened the spear tips and the rock to the downed quill bole. He managed to lift it enough to pull his leg out from under it. Blood soaked his pantleg where one of the carved quill spears protruded from his right calf. The pain was intense and he struggled to control his breath. He found a long stick and used it as a crutch to lift himself to his feet. There was no other option but to slowly hobble back to the oxygen trap.

As he limped forward, darkness began to eat at the edges of Liam's vision. The world narrowed as if he were back at the cottage looking through the eyepiece of the telescope. Things appeared much closer than they were. The oxygen trap was a large pin prick in the distance.

He collapsed through the trap's flap and nearly fell through to the other side. He landed on the grill that covered the hole and, with shaking hands, sealed the trap from the inside as best he could. He laid on his back, the side of his face pressed against the grill, breathing, hyperventilating. He was confused and terrified and blind.

Though the darkness remained, his vision slowly returned. He saw the twenty-centimetre wooden fang in his leg and knew he'd have to pull it out as soon as possible. He cut out his Snuggie's front pocket and found the roll of duct tape. He'd need to be quick. He cut the leg off his pants with the knife. Blood seeped out from around the fang. He pulled on it hard and the pain escaped his control. A dark river of crimson welled up from the wound, and Liam pressed the pocket's fabric to it and taped as tightly as he could. He was numb. Dizzy. And then he passed out.

\*\*\*

*You're doing so well, my lovely. Get some rest. Everything's going to be alright. Go to sleep. It's okay. Shhhhhh. Allow yourself to relax. There you go. You got this, my lovely. You deserve rest. You are loved. Loved. Be gentle to yourself. Be kind. I'm so proud of you. Sleep. I left you something, my lovely. Just be gentle. Relax. Go to sleep. Don't worry, everything will be fine. It's okay. Good. There you go. You're doing such a good job.*

\*\*\*

*A healthy, well-nourished person can physically tolerate a great deal, provided that they have confidence. Even if sick or injured, a determined person can win through and recover from seemingly impossible situations.*

Blood had soaked through Liam's make-shift bandage, yet it staunched any additional bleeding. The pain was constant, but he was alive. He resisted the desire to remove the bandage, fearing what he'd see. More blood. Infection. Or worse. He had no idea how long he'd been unconscious. He was pale, anemic. His skin had taken on a blue hue. He needed water. And food. That's not all you need, thought Liam. You need a miracle.

Liam moved, tentatively. He'd have many hours, days, weeks maybe, to become intimate with the contours of his pain. The promise of it, knowing that it could only get worse, was overwhelming. He pulled himself into a sitting position, his injured leg stretched out before him. It was a small relief to be off the grill. It was then that he noticed a golden drawstring, tied in a prusik knot, on one of the thin charcoal-dipped metal rods of the barbeque grill. A bag, the purple crown royal bag, hung below it. He removed the rocks and tent pegs and flipped over the grill. He loosened the drawstring and saw that inside was a fist-sized nut: a seed; a giant sapseed.

He opened the survival handbook to the section on sapseeds.

*The giant sapseed, like all members of the sapseed genus, are highly evolved parasites. Their root network is extensive, and they will frequently graft to neighbouring plants and use them as a source of carbohydrates and nutrients, which are concentrated in their sap. Sap production can be voluminous and is an excellent source of nutrition. Their seeds are highly poisonous.*

As if reacting to his disappointment, pain radiated throughout his body. Liam held his breath until it passed. He needed medical supplies, not a seed, and they were, stupidly, he recognized, at the cottage. A five-minute walk from the den and oxygen trap. Likely more, given his injury. The best he could do, which seemed ill-advised, was to make what the survival handbook called an oxygen backpack: in essence, a bag of air.

Liam assessed the hole before him. He opened a garbage bag and ran his hand from bottom to top to expel as much air as possible, then held the open end to the hole, sealing it as tightly as he could. It was a slow process, but when the bag was filled, he tied it tight and opened the trap's flap to push the bag outside. He did this two more times until he had filled them all with what he hoped was enough oxygen to get him to the cottage and back.

Liam tied two of the bags to the quill stick he used as a crutch, held the other in his free hand, and began the slow descent down the path that led to the cottage;

through hiss nettles, out of the quills, stopping too frequently to breathe in a lungful of bagged oxygen. Going down the hill would be the easy part, thought Liam. Three bags started to seem like too light a load.

Aside from the additional splatfern that had fallen on its roof, the cottage looked much the same. Liam breathed in the last of the oxygen from the first bag, squeezing it into a ball before carefully, slowly, climbing the steps that led to the door.

Inside, Liam wasted little time. He went to the linen closet and removed the wicker basket holding the medical supplies and a bottle of ibuprofen. He found scissors and gauze and bandages. He cut through the duct tape and peeled off the bloody rags, which had become stuck to the wound. It gave off a foul smell; after covering it with hydrogen peroxide and swabbing it clean, Liam saw that there remained a dark-coloured corona of decaying flesh. He feared gangrene had set in. He pressed a ball of gauze against the hole and covered it with the bandage and taped it in place. He swallowed four ibuprofen tablets and put everything into the expended garbage bag.

Liam huffed from the second bag.

He climbed to the second floor, to the bedroom and the gun case inside it. The climb was slow and painful, and by the time he reached the case and had it opened on the bed, the second oxygen bag was a little more than half-full. Half-empty, corrected Liam. He collected as many .22 bullets as he could find and stuffed them in his pocket. Above him, the once azure skylight had been dissolved by splatfern.

Liam left the cottage, possibly for the last time, and began his measured ascent up the hill. Each step brought fresh new pain. He inhaled greedily from the third – and final – bag. Albeit woozy and light-headed, Liam stopped to collect several sun tails, their stalks filled with juice. He added them to the bag of medical supplies, which he threw back over his shoulder. He staggered the way back, dropped the supplies outside the den and fell into the oxygen trap. Inside, he gasped in fits and gulped down the invisible ambrosia contained within.

Somewhat recovered, Liam retrieved the bag of supplies. He chewed on the stalks of sun tails and swallowed four more ibuprofen. His wound bled through the new bandage.

*Fire has been used for centuries to clean wounds. Cauterising with heat requires fortitude for the patient – but, if they can stand it, and you have ammunition, placing powder around a wound and lighting it can prevent gangrene. Know that the shock of this on top of the shock of the injury will kill some people.*

Liam removed the bullets from his pockets. Twelve in total. With the tip of his knife, he loosened one bullet from its case. It was a slow and frustrating process, but once he had the one out, he used its empty casing, sliding it on top of a live round, bending the two to loosen and work the bullet out. The amount of powder he collected was less than he imagined it would be.

He went outside, sealing the trap's flap behind him, and sat. He removed the bandage, poured peroxide on the wound, and watched it bubble and patted it dry. He tore open and folded a loratadine box into a V-shape and transferred the dry powder into it. Cautiously, he traced the necrotic outline that had begun to circle the puncture wound, hopeful that when lit the grains wouldn't fall into the wound itself.

He bit on his crutch and clicked the barbeque lighter on, its small flame barely visible, and he held it to the powder.

The pain separated him from his body. Someone, somewhere, was screaming. It was all he could do to pull himself inside before the darkness returned.

\*\*\*

A tongue licked his face. Went over his closed eyes and nose and lapped at his ears, then went into his mouth. Under his lips. The tongue explored the texture of his teeth and gums and then went down his throat. Into the esophagus. Its taste buds absorbed the acidity of his stomach. It ran along his stomach's walls, into the pylorus. Testing, sensing, analyzing. And then retracted out of his body like a tape measure.

A radio played. An alien language.

More appendages, tendrils, flopped across Liam's delirious body. His mind retreated into itself. Sapped of function. He watched without seeing. Felt without feeling. Thought without thinking.

"...the new reconciliation tax. We'd like to make this a permanent program and I don't think it shouldn't be optional anymore. All of us benefit from the wealth generated on our asteroids, and the courts have said that, you know, and so now the nadanians can benefit from them too. And that's what the tax will do. It's encouraging to see people volunteer toward reconciliation, but I don't know if that's enough. Look at the wealth they're getting from being on our asteroids..."

Long tubes uncoiled and grew into every orifice of Liam's body. Up his nose. Into his stomach. Through his anus. Bladder. They fed. Collected. Ate. As they grew, Liam's body was elevated from below. Buttressed. Held. Caressed.

"...when nadanians signed treaty, what were we given? A pittance. Treaty said $5 a year. What does that buy now? The Universal Government needs to fix this. And meanwhile, what have we got in return? Nothing. The government needs to account for inflation because it hasn't changed for, what, like, hundreds of years. We're seeking compensation for this, $10 billion, because things like this, they shouldn't have happened..."

A mouth sucked on Liam's wound. Kissed it. Swallowed pus and purulence. Spat on it. Smeared it in sap.

"...the soil, it remembers us, us nadanians, it doesn't remember you humanians. And the soil, the land, the asteroid, it knows who the real title holders are, it calls to us, it whispers to us from generation to generation. It remembers, you see. The asteroid's blood remembers us. That's why we have to reclaim it. Every asteroid. They're ours, you know. That's why we have to be in control. Because right now, it's out of control. That's why the Universal Government adopted the declaration on the rights of nadanians, because of those bodies they found, the bodies of little ones. But the Universal Government, they don't know how to look after the land..."

Liam stirred, yet consciousness remained distant. The radio, indifferent to his suffering, continued nonetheless.

"...significant decision. The Gar-Nadan government has issued a quill harvest licence to the Nadnano Nation. Nadnano Nation acquired harvesting rights to the area after the Nada Quill Company failed to address the community's concerns. Nada Quill Company had been operating in Gar-Nada since 280PC and was unsuccessful in its application to renew. The Nadnano Nation say that the revenue brought in from quill harvesting will be used to address their community's needs..."

"'These are sacred asteroids,' said Ahkeh Johnson. 'It's our right to have control over how these resources are used. No one else can tell us how to use our ancestral asteroids. And now that we hold the licence, we can harvest quills in a way that respects the great sapper...'"

Liam's eyes fluttered. His consciousness crept back into him. It was the project he'd been fired over. The Nada Quill Company. The licence had not been denied. It had gone to the community. The community who had complained about how every quill had a spirit and couldn't be cut down had suddenly embraced their harvest.

"'...it's about economic reconciliation, and it's about damn time. These companies have been operating on our land for far too long...'"

Both the radio and Liam's tortured mind fell silent.

*Renault Decision, 353PC. The case involved the Renault treaty, made with Suun nadanians prior to the nadanian treaty. At issue was whether the annual annuity promise in the Renault treaty was required to be periodic updated; as well, they demanded a share of the revenues generated from resource development on surrendered asteroids. The Universal Government agreed to pay the Suun nation $10 billion. The decision has been used as precedent for similar claims throughout Nada.*

# 10

How long Liam slept, he hadn't a clue. How long had he lain there while the roots of the giant sapseed kept him alive? How long had they nourished him? Fed and watered him? Breathed for him? A week, a month, a year?

The oxygen trap was gone. A piece of it, looking like a shredded black plastic flag, hung limply from a featherless quill bole.

The den was gone, too. In its place, which seemed to emerge from the hole, filling it, was the base of a giant sapseed. It was alive. From there, it hadn't grown straight; instead, it angled sharply toward its long-dead ancestor, penetrating its bark, growing inside its protective shell. Its crown, like a large and many-fingered hand, extended beyond the dead sleeve of its hollow relative. It was at that crook near the sapseed's base where Liam had slept, cradled in a bed of bark and roots – where, of the sapseed's curious will, rhizomes or tendrils or filamentous tubes had entered Liam's body. A layer of grey dust had settled over everything. Liam's chest rose and fell, and the dust on his Snuggie rose and fell with it.

Had he been dreaming? Were they peaceful dreams? Or had Liam's mind simply turned off, hijacked perhaps, its duties momentarily reassigned, entered into a long period of nothingness, where time and space were insubstantial, where before and after had no meaning, where the self and the other had no clear distinction.

Even so, nothing can't last forever. Liam opened his eyes.

He coughed, struggled for air, instinctively pulled out the long vegetative tubes that had grown into his lungs and stomach and large intestine. They came out with ribbons of bile and mucus, muted and wet popping sounds, and flopped to the dusty ground, where they writhed like white worms.

Liam gasped for air and breathed with an ease he barely recognized. He leaned forward unsteadily, his muscles weak from disuse.

Around him, the quills were dead. The knot and feather quills. The jelly quills. The punchplants that hung from them like beards. The understorey, too, was dead. Sun tails and canker moss. Jam roots and pipe fingers. Hareberries. Bullet berries. Hiss nettles. Horn bladders and bracketworts. Ratfruit and pickle vine and cutweed. All dead. Their shriveled corpses littered the landscape. Everywhere: a grey dust.

Liam pushed himself off the sapseed's elbowed bole and stood beside it, skeptical of his ability to stand without support, and took two tentative steps.

There were no footprints, no tracks through the dust. No scat bears or quill slugs. No rain eels hid in the brush, there was no longer any brush to hide amongst. No swat fleas buzzed above him. No cone lice floated in swarms in the liminal space of the cloudlake. No blackfish shimmered. No cloud crabs swam. No sign of molerin or spiner. The silence was thick. Nothing.

All that remained alive, aside from Liam himself, was the giant sapseed. It loomed over everything else. Its bulbous, drooping flowers hung like flaccid trumpets. Its fruit was enormous, many the size of basketballs; the largest was the size of a small car. Each held by a massive wooden limb.

Liam found the buck knife and radio under a skin of grey dust. He cranked the radio's handle, turned the tuning dial, and heard only static.

He walked down the trail to Seven Breezes. The cottage had slumped in on itself. The front steps and much of the deck were coated in the long-dead remnants of splatfern, their dried shadows looked burned into the weakened timber.

Liam peered through the doorway. Walls were buckled. Shattered glass littered the floor. The contents of the upstairs bedroom had collapsed into the kitchen and living room. A stale smell pervaded the destruction. Liam doubted the floor would hold his weight.

He walked to the shore, to the edge of the cloudlake. Merlan's asteroid was empty. Seidelskyys', too, looked barren. There was nothing left. Even the sky seemed dead.

He returned to the giant sapseed and kicked around in the dust. He found some pages from the survival handbook. There was no handbook for this, thought Liam. Only death.

The giant sapseed above was like a ladder to the distant stars. Its generous branches spanned the dark sky, as if triumphant, as if it were proud to be the lone survivor, as if that was its sole existential intent. Great tears of sap dripped from its bole. Liam grabbed one of the tears and an amber honey melted in his palm. He ate the teardrop as he would an apple. Its moist sweetness was warm and sad.

When night arrived, Liam watched the stars that rested just beyond the sapseed's boughs. He saw the constellation of the great sapper spread out before him, each one like a strawberry mark. He saw the neck of the universe, its lithe shoulders, its belly button and breasts. Liam stared at the star just below Dolly's nipple. Somewhere in that direction was Rock Nippan, and a little beyond that was Rock Islin, and Jenn. It'd been so long since he'd heard her voice, since he'd seen and held her.

The universe was not made for life. It was a wasteland. Nothing survived its cruelty, its ignorant sadism, its lack of shame or remorse. That's the truth, as Liam saw it. There was nothing for him here. And he couldn't just leave, could he?

Liam pulled out the damaged and dusty page from his pocket.

*...and then one* rides the seed; *the phrase has also come to mean to* leave, *to* ramble *or* wander, *to* look for better days *or* toward the future, *and, in many nadanian cultures, it also means to...*

To die, Liam finished. The words seemed to float before him. They fused with the sky's strawberry marks, with Jenn and Rock Nippan, with Seven Breezes, with the lifeless distance between them all.

Liam waited until the diffuse light of day returned before he climbed into the crown of the giant sapseed. He used his knife for leverage, stabbing as he climbed, and pulled himself up, and from each cut he made there oozed from it the plant's divine sap. From what Liam could remember from the survival handbook, although the accuracy of it hardly mattered now, a small hole was to be cut in the side of a large, yet still immature, fruit, large enough for a person – a nadanian, traditionally – to squeeze through. The flesh inside would need to be carved out, but not all of it; like sap, it was edible and nutritious. As the fruit ripened, its once-soft skin would harden, and a pressure would mount behind its base.

Liam carved into the largest of the fruits, which, he thought, seemed to be pointed toward the Rock Nippan star. A short blast of oxygen greeted the knife's blade as he pushed it in, and Liam scooped out its flesh, tossing handfuls of it to the ground.

Nothing happened while he waited for the fruit to dry. He ate its moist flesh. He drank its sweet and watery sap. He walked to the cottage and back. He walked to the south end and back. He saw nothing and nothing saw him. He slept dreamlessly. He heard no whispers. The radio continued to play only static. Liam remembered that the static was the sound of the birth of the universe, and he kept it on at night to hear its wailings. It, too, was the sound of death, he thought gloomily.

And then one day Liam climbed the giant sapseed for the last time. As he did, he went by one of the plant's large drooping flowers. Its white petals sagged like popped balloons. He peeled one of them back and saw, not just one or two, but hundreds of rainbow fleas. Their tiny bodies seemed overjoyed to be discovered. They bathed in the flower's pollen, their tiny tube-mouths sucked up a fragrant nectar; they danced and flitted and hopped excitedly around its multiple pistils. Long ago, he could have watched them dance for hours.

Instead, Liam gently returned the petal to its place and continued his ascent into the crown where the fruit had, by then, hardened to a rock-like shell. He descended into the hole and, once inside, pulled on its tightly fitted cover to close it. He smeared a paste of sap into the seams where it would dry and seal him in.

Liam then lay in its darkness and breathed.

And waited to ride the seed.

# Epilogue

The only part of the story that's true was near its beginning: *Ahmem can do whatever he wants whenever he wants.* The rest of it is a lie.

And even so, my name isn't Ahmem. It's true that people have called me that, nadanians even, but that doesn't make it the truth. I am not defined by a name. I am not defined by a narrative. I am defined by the truth.

And that, my friend, is the truth I'm trying to tell you. Because without the truth, what else have you got?

Nothing. Nix. Nowt. Zip. Zilch. Zero.

Nada.

Call it whatever you like. But don't you dare call it the truth, lady.

www.ingramcontent.com/pod-product-compliance
Lightning Source LLC
LaVergne TN
LVHW020447070526
838199LV00063B/4868